D0573720

EMBROIDERED GARDENS

HOW TO USE THIS BOOK

Embroidered Gardens has been designed as a book to be used. The final chapter, Ideas for Embroidering Gardens, shows how to work some of the embroidery techniques that were in use from the sixteenth century to the present. The chapter gives details of the fabric, thread and stitches to use in the embroidery of each century, as well as providing general information on materials and techniques and showing how to enlarge and reduce designs.

Throughout the book, motifs taken from contemporary embroidery and garden books are shown in the margins, providing a source of patterns which can be arranged and embroidered in many different ways. The knots and mazes of blackwork, the amusing stumpwork animals and insects and the geometric patterns of Berlin woolwork are all there to embroider.

This book was designed and produced by
Martensson Books, London

Managing editor	Wendy Martensson
Editor	Pamela Tubby
Art director	Erica Matlow
Art assistant	Gillian Whitlock
Photography	Chris Overton
Illustrations	Marion Appleton
	Gillian Chapman

Published in 1979 by The Viking Press
625 Madison Avenue, New York, N.Y. 10022

Published simultaneously in Canada by
Penguin Books Canada Limited

Library of Congress catalog card number: 78-68812

ISBN 0-670-29260-5

Printed in Hong Kong

EMBROIDERED GARDENS

Thomasina Beck

A STUDIO BOOK
THE VIKING PRESS · NEW YORK

In Spring, when Flowr's your garden grace,
With Needle or Pencil you can trace
Each curious Form, and various Dye
So represent unto the Eye,
Noble proportion ev'ry part
That Nature blushes at your Art.
John Rea, *Flora,* 1665

An interest in gardens and embroidery often tends to go together, and in this book I have tried to show some of the links between them. The gardens and embroideries are described whenever possible in the words of contemporary writers whose evidence together with the illustrations, show how each art reveals in the other similar themes, patterns and moods.

I was not interested in gardens until I had one of my own. It was a small neglected London garden and I was given much needed advice on improvements by Roland Preece, a gifted gardener whose knowledge and love of plants was reflected in the embroidery that occupied every moment of his spare time. I admired his work and he offered to teach me some simple stitches beginning with tent stitch in a pattern of fleur de lys.

My interest in gardening grew and I began reading garden books and visiting other peoples' gardens. At much the same time I started studying embroidery with Joan Edwards at the Royal School of Needlework. She taught me to look at embroidery in the widest possible context and I am very much indebted to her for all her help and encouragement.

I should also like to thank Mrs Madeleine Mainstone, Keeper of Education at the Victoria and Albert Museum for giving me the chance to teach in her department. Many of the ideas in the book were evolved while thinking out lectures for students in the museum.

My thanks are also due to Wendy Martensson whose enthusiasm for the pictures convinced me that I should try to write about them, Erica Matlow who designed the book so skilfully, and Pamela Tubby who worked out the practicalities of my suggestions for embroidered gardens.

Christopher Thacker answered endless questions on the garden aspect of my theme and I am more grateful than I can say for his patient and generous help.

Thomasina Beck London 1978

Contents

ELIZABETHAN GARDENS

All is work and nowhere space

Thomas Campion
from Philip Rosseter's "A Book of Airs", 1601

ROMANCY PLEASANT PLACES

"For if delight may provoke men's labour, what greater delight is there than to behold the earth apparelled with plants, as with a robe of imbroidered works, set with orient pearles and garnished with great diversitie of rare and costly jewels." John Gerard wrote this in 1597 dedicating his *Herball* to Lord Burghley. Gerard had supervised the great statesman's magnificent gardens at Theobalds near London and his comparison of the decorative effect of embroidered dress with a profusion of growing plants could have been inspired either by the beauty of Lord Burghley's famous flower collection or by the variety of plants which Gerard himself grew in his own simple plot a few miles away in Holborn.

In the sixteenth century many writers and poets noted a resemblance between their gardens and the embroidery around them, and they would have known exactly what Gerard meant. Their gardens had rare, ornate and fanciful qualities which found a real and extraordinary parallel in the embroidery of the period. Each art then reached a perfection which has hardly been surpassed in later years—though succeeding fashions may have overshadowed their achievements. Since hardly a trace of these gardens remains for us to visit—all were destroyed or submerged in the following centuries—the surviving embroideries are not only examples of one art but a precious record of another; the two being strangely and wonderfully related and between them evoking the aesthetic and mysterious images of the age.

Elizabethan embroidery resembled the garden in two distinct ways. Miniature garden scenes illustrating all the features then in fashion were depicted in embroidered furnishings where every detail of the layout was clear except for the actual planting in the beds. The tiny scale of these embroideries makes it impossible to see which plants were used and how they were arranged. The plants can, however, be seen in detail on "robes of imbroidered work" and other embroideries where they were arranged to create decorative effects similar to those in the garden. Herein lay the second resemblance.

The miniature scenes appeared most often in the background of luxurious furnishings which were among the most exciting decorative innovations of the age. The gardens can be seen in hangings, cushions, table carpets—carpets on the floor were a rarity seen only in the grandest houses—and valances. Valances were long bands of canvaswork made in sets of three to hang from the roof of a four-poster bed. They were ideal for narrative embroidery where the story unfolds in a series of episodes. Fortunes were spent on bed hangings; and when garden scenes were worked on the valances and bright flowers ran riot on

pillows, coverlets and curtains, the whole bed echoed the garden. This may have been in Christopher Marlowe's mind when he described the interweaving of honeysuckle and rose stems over a stream as being like embroidery: "and as a costly valance o'er a bed, So did their garland tops the brook o'er spread."
The furnishings were embroidered in tent stitch in silk or wool on fine linen canvas, and many of them were produced in professional workrooms where several embroiderers could sit round a large frame. They transformed the interiors of Elizabethan houses, making them brighter and more inviting than ever before. The embroideries were especially appealing to their owners because they brought echoes of the garden indoors to be enjoyed throughout the year, preserving flowers and sunshine, spring and summer to brighten the gloomy winter days. The gardens were not the main subject of the furnishings, but were again and again the setting for a varied cast of biblical, mythological and allegorical characters, acting out scenes from a distant legendary past while incongruously dressed in the height of current fashion. Details of the dress may often suggest a French origin for the figures were frequently copied from French or Flemish engravings. The copying was done by a professional draughtsman, who would enliven the foreground with an array of small animals and individual plants, and fill in the background around the figures with contemporary garden scenes. Here the fashions in France and England remained remarkably similar

Elizabethan garden features appear in miniature in many late sixteenth century embroidered furnishings. Top: Fountain, pool and carpenter's work in a garden possibly representing the old Palace of Hatfield where the young Princess Elizabeth is seen with her stepmother Catherine Parr and her tutor Roger Ascham. Bottom: Musical garden party.

throughout the sixteenth century. If they were specially commissioned, their future owner may sometimes have asked for the scene to include a view or a glimpse of his own garden, just as his coat of arms might be incorporated into some part of the design.

Although the gardens no longer exist, vivid contemporary descriptions record them at the height of their glory. Garden visiting was as popular then as it is now, and a German named Paul Hentzner, who visited the gardens of Henry VIII's fantastic palace at Nonsuch in 1598, records that it was "so encompassed with parks full of verdure, deer, delicious gardens, groves ornamented with trelliswork, and cabinets of verdure that it seems to be a place pitched upon by Pleasure to dwell in along with Health." A year later another traveller, Thomas Platter, also went to Nonsuch where he found Queen Elizabeth in residence. The party were conducted to the Presence Chamber, saw the Queen "most lavishly attired in a gown of pure white satin, gold embroidered," and then after dining, walked amid the mazes and knots in the garden.

Knots were beds laid out in elaborate patterns, planted in low clipped evergreens where "all kinds of plants and shrubs are mingled in intricate circles as though by the needle of Semiramis." The comparison is apt, for inside the great houses the travellers visited, they would have seen tapestries and embroidered furnishings of all kinds. Many of them depicted gardens and were so finely wrought that they might indeed have been the work of Semiramis, the legendary Eastern queen famous for the splendour of her gardens. The embroidered scenes correspond in every detail with the written accounts and, according to Platter, were so lifelike that "the plants seemed to be growing indeed." Platter also visited Hampton Court and saw "extremely costly tapestries worked in gold and silver and silk so lifelike that one might take the people and plants for real."

Sometimes the garden theme was continued in painting as at Theobalds where the walls of the Great Chamber were decorated with oak trees so startlingly realistic that birds flew in singing from the pleasure gardens outside to perch on the branches. Indoors seemed to be masquerading as outdoors and vice versa. The effect was delightfully ambiguous as Barnaby Googe remarked enthusiastically in 1577. "Your Parlers, and your banketting houses both within and without, as all bedecked with pictures of beautiful Flowres and Trees, that you may not onley feede your eyes with the beholding of the true and lively flowre, but also delight your selfe with the counterfaite in the middest of Winter."

The garden in the Franklin hanging shown on page 13, records in miniature the features the travellers actually saw. A hunting park stretches away into woodland behind the house, while in complete contrast to the park, the garden lies peaceful and serene. It is like the transformation John Aubrey noted when he wrote that Lord Stourton had, in making his garden,

Opposite: Title page of Gerard's Herball *of 1597 ornamented with a "delectable variety" of new plant introductions as well as old favourites such as roses and pinks. The layout of small neat beds in the garden of the cartouche at the bottom of the page is often repeated in the background of narrative embroideries. Below: Valance telling the story of Tobias and the angel, Tobias takes leave of his father outside the trellis fence of a garden whose tiny regular beds are enclosed by an alley in carpenter's work.*

The Metropolitan Museum of Art, Gift of Irwin Untermeyer, 1964

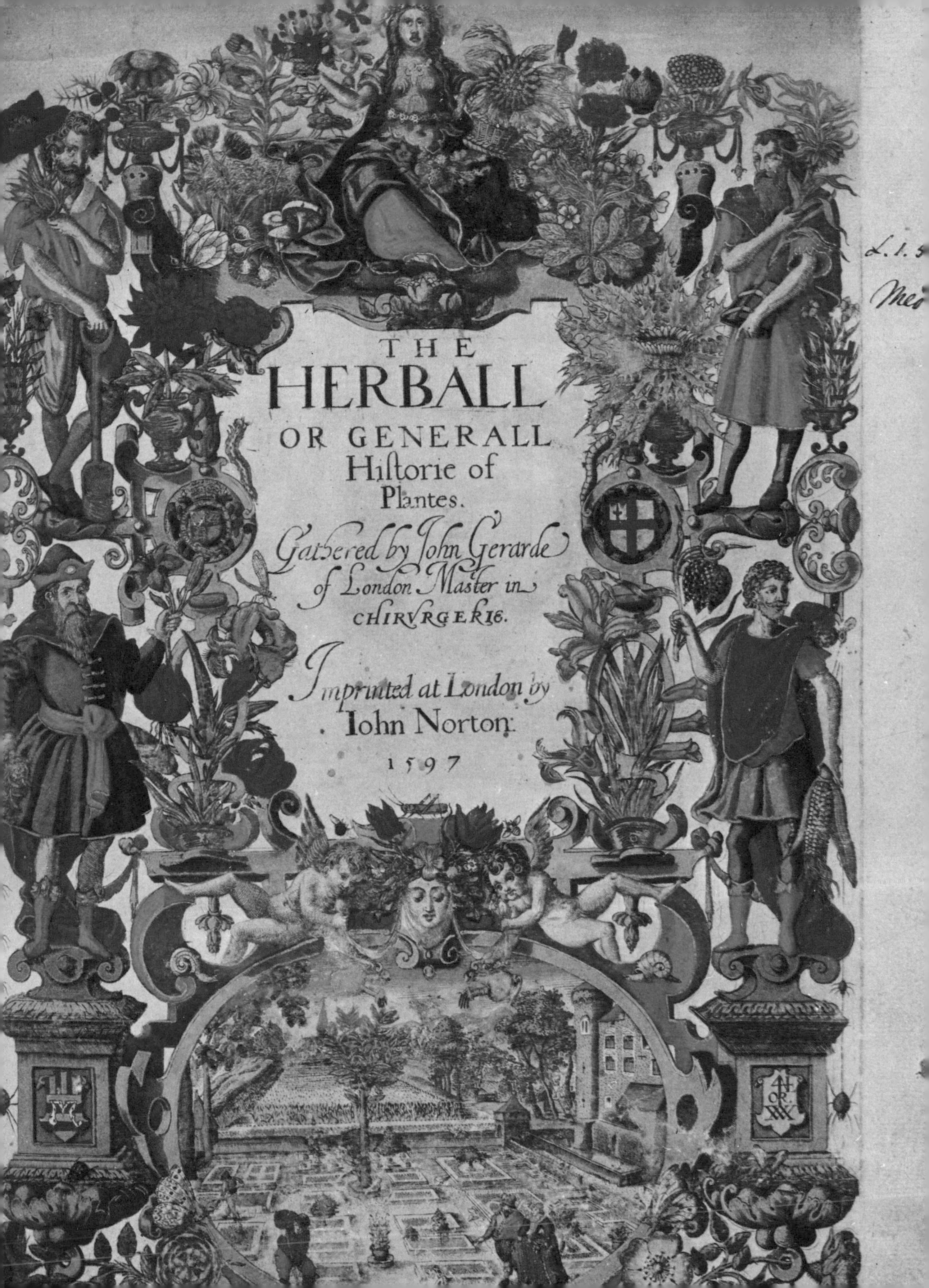
THE
HERBALL
OR GENERALL
Historie of
Plantes.
Gathered by John Gerarde
of London Master in
CHIRURGERIE.
Imprinted at London by
Iohn Norton.
1597
L. 1. 5
Meo

Above: Detail from a valance of the story of Adonis and Myrrah. Myrrah and her nurse meet in the privacy of a knot garden whose layout closely resembles the woodcut (shown left) on the title page of Thomas Hill's A Most Brief and Pleasant Treatyse. *Opposite: Detail from a valance with a couple seated in a rose arbour on a trellis framework like the one on the right in the woodcut. The plants for arbours were described in* The Country Farm: "*The Garden of Pleasure shall be set about and compassed with arbors made of jessamin, rosemarie, box, juniper, cypress-trees, savin, cedars, rose-trees and other dainties first planted and pruned according as the nature of every one doth require, but after brought into some form and order with willow or juniper poles, such as may serve for the making of arbors.*" *Gardeners using juniper poles to construct an arbour can be seen on page 19.*

converted what was "heretofore all horrid and woody" into "a most parkly ground and romancy pleasant place." Here, nature is dressed up as ornately and corseted as stiffly as the ladies and gentlemen in the foreground, with the garden designed to set off the house as elaborately as the ruffs framing the faces of its owners. In the garden there are circular mazes planted with evergreen shrubs and herbs like santolina, lavender and thrift, whose complexity was best appreciated when viewed from the windows or the terrace of the house. Richard Surflet in *The Country Farm* published in 1600 describes his joy at looking over his garden seeing "fair and comely proportions, handsome and pleasant arbours, and as it were closets, delightful borders of lavendar, rosemary, box and other such like" and smelling "so sweet a nosegay so near at hand."

Opposite: The Elizabethan garden at Cranborne Manor, Dorset. The box-edged beds are planted with a charming miscellany of spring flowers including many small bulbs to create the effect of a mixed nosegay. Below: The Franklin hanging. The garden lies behind the house, its round mazes, elaborate pavilions and fountain making a sophisticated contrast to the hunting park and the countryside beyond.

FROM CLOISTER TO PLEASURE GARDEN

The Elizabethan gardens had all the charm of novelty. Visitors even a century before would have seen nothing like them in the turbulent days before Tudor rule. There were gardens then of course, but they were hidden away behind the walls of castles and monasteries, where herbs were grown for medicinal or culinary purposes. Flowers were for the decoration of the church and for weaving into garlands on festival days. The simple layout of these early gardens, with a neat chequerboard of raised beds, fountains and covered walks, can be seen small and jewel-like in illuminated manuscripts and books of hours.

The concept of the English country house as the centre of an agreeable and leisurely way of life came into being in the sixteenth century and the garden was to play an important part in the process. The Elizabethan garden as depicted in the valance on page 14 retained the main features of the medieval cloister garden. The plan is still close to the cruciform layout in the cloister with a fountain at the centre and a carefully trained leafy tunnel with a wooden frame, called "carpenter's work", round the sides. But in castle and monastery it would have been further enclosed

by a high wall so that it was shut in on itself and as inward looking as the world of which it was a part. Now the house looks peacefully out over the garden and on to the countryside beyond, and the owner might see pleasant views of each as he walked in the shade of the alley and paused at one of its openings. The leafy alleys which go round the three sides of the square are wholly characteristic of Elizabethan gardens.

Thomas Hill's *The Gardeners Labyrinth* of 1577 expresses the delight of Renaissance gardeners in the new-found pleasure of their gardens. "The commodities of these Alleis and walks serve to good purposes, the one is that the owner may diligently view the prosperitie of his herbes and flowers, the other for the delight and comfort of his wearied mind, which he may by himself or in fellowship of his friendes conceyve, in the delectable sightes and fragrant smelles of the flowers."

"This little river encompassing the Garden doth wonderfully set it forth, and here the greene and goodly quickset Hedges defendeth it both from Man and Beast" Barnaby Googe. Valance detail.

Without gardens, "buildings and palaces are but gross handiworks: and a man shall ever see that when ages come to civility and elegancy, men come to build stately sooner than to garden finely; as if gardening were the greater perfection," wrote Lord Bacon in his essay *On Gardens,* published in 1625. Himself as much an Elizabethan as a Jacobean—he was born in 1561—Bacon was expressing Elizabethan sentiments exactly, for people then had no doubts about their "civility and elegancy," and the garden was ideal for showing off both qualities.

Like their clothes and their houses, the garden was a status symbol reflecting not only the owner's taste and wealth, but also his own creative talent in a novel and pleasingly idiosyncratic manner. The owners of the new mansions that were being built all over England were enthusiastically involved in the arts. They read widely, wrote, composed, sang and danced. They supervised the building, and sometimes even designed their houses themselves, and indulged their taste for intricate patterning and elaborate effects in every detail of the decoration. Gardening became an accomplishment as well as being a pastime—an enthusiasm which became a passion—and at exactly the same time embroidery, which had long been a necessary accomplishment, began to flourish with a new exuberance. Together, garden and embroidery combined to add the perfect finishing touch to the house and its contents.

For those who, despite their "civility and elegancy," were not quite sure how to go about the practical side of laying out a garden and cultivating plants, books soon began to appear. The first was by Thomas Hill, author of *The Gardeners Labyrinth.* It was published in 1563, and entitled *A Most Briefe and pleasant treatyse, teachynge howe to dress, sowe and set a Garden, and what propertyes also these few herbes heare spoken of, have to our comodytie: with the remedyes that may be used against such beasts, wormes, flies and such lyke, that commonly noy gardens, gathered out of the principallest Authors in this art.* The many "beasts, wormes, flies and such lyke" in Elizabethan embroidery suggest that the "remedyes" were seldom successful.

THE ROMANCE OF THE VALANCE

On Hill's title page there is a tiny woodcut of a garden set in the countryside yet enclosed on all four sides and symmetrically divided within. Its privacy and seclusion, its detailed layout and its rural situation are typical of the Elizabethan garden and all are repeated in a pair of valances telling the double and linked stories of Adonis and Myrrah, and Venus and Adonis from Ovid's *Metamorphoses*.

The story opens with the dramatic image of Myrrah on the point of hanging herself in an arbour well hidden by a luxuriant vine trained on trellis between flower-bedecked columns. The well-read Elizabethan would have known at once that the cause of Myrrah's distress was her incestuous passion for her father who had unwisely boasted that his daughter's beauty rivalled that of the goddess Venus. Myrrah's old nurse leads her from the arbour into the knot garden, and in a secluded corner outlines her plan; while his wife is away, she will make Myrrah's father drink a potion so that he sleeps with his own daugher unknowingly. When he discovers Myrrah is pregnant her father chases her from the house; just as he is about to strike her with his sword Venus relents and turns her into a tree whose gaping trunk reveals the baby Adonis. This second valance is much closer in theme to the two poems in which Shakespeare talks of the legend, *The Passionate Pilgrim* and *Venus and Adonis*. Neither the tale on the valances nor the poems are deeply learned, but the embroiderer has seized upon this story of thwarted amorous dalliance—an apt and intentional choice of subject for bed hangings—for the excuse it provides to depict the pleasures and trials of love in a setting of rural and garden delight. In the

Detail of the story of Philomena whose tongue has been cut out by the King of Thrace. In a garden setting she embroiders a message for her sister warning her of a similar fate.

The Metropolitan Museum of Art, Gift of Irwin Untermeyer, 1964

The Metropolitan Museum of Art, Gift of Irwin Untermeyer, 1964

A pair of valances linking the stories of Myrrah and Adonis, and Venus and Adonis. Top: The first two episodes take place in a vine arbour and knot garden. Bottom: Adonis encounters the boar and is killed in a setting continuing the garden theme with a fountain fed by a stream and a small snail-shaped mount to the left of Venus seen driving her chariot through the clouds.

second story, Adonis, now a young man, "lovely and fresh and green," has disdained the advances of Venus choosing rather to go out hunting. In the valance he meets and is killed by a wild boar, "a fair sweet youth Here in these brakes deep wounded with a boar." But the valances change the forest "brakes" to an orchard beside an ornate marble fountain with a stream running between flowery banks. Venus and her attendants kneel round the dead Adonis while a nightingale laments in the tree behind. Two details in the background continue the garden setting—far to the rear there is a sumptuous summer house similar perhaps to the one "pleasantly situated upon the highest part of Nonsuch Park" from which the guests might view the hunt; and just adjacent to Venus in the clouds, there is a tiny snail-shaped mount.

Mounts, made from earth, wood or stone "harmonously wrought within and without" were small artificial hillocks raised up in the garden, either against the outer wall, or in the centre, and they might also be topped by an arbour or even a banqueting house. Whether in the centre or against the wall, they were vantage points from which to see beyond the garden into park and countryside or to look down onto the patterns in the knotted beds.

Mounts are rare in the embroidered garden but the one in the Adonis valance is certainly close to the description of a mount with topiary work seen by John Leland at Wressel Castle in the 1540's, "writhen about with degrees like turnings of cokilshells to come to the top without payne." It is also similar to the strange floating "snail mount" constructed to take part in the water pageant on the lake at Elvetham where Lord Hertford entertained Queen Elizabeth in 1591. The Queen sat in a large bower decorated with greenery and ripe hazel nuts on a bank above the lake which had been created especially for the revels during which—in true English fashion—"it rained extremely."

MANY DELIGHTS OF RARE INVENTION

Although she did not herself make any new gardens, the Queen's summer progresses into the country to visit her courtiers made them vie with each other, not only in building lavish houses but also

The Metropolitan Museum of Art, Gift of Irwin Untermeyer, 1964

"Silver sounding Musick, mixt instruments and voices gracing all the rest: How you will be wrapt with Delight." Music and dancing were favourite summer entertainments in Elizabethan and Jacobean gardens. Late sixteenth century valance. In the detail below, an alley in carpenter's work provides refreshing shade and frames the views over the four-square plot.

in creating gardens which set the scene for masques and revels, for music and dancing, bathing and all kinds of sports and games. In fine weather all social activity migrated to the garden which was decked out to match the mood of the entertainments.

The embroidered gardens seem able to catch this atmosphere of gaiety and pleasure more evocatively than the simple, rather crude woodcuts illustrating contemporary books or the few paintings that survive. One reason may be that embroidery and tapestry have in their texture a quality of depth and softness and warmth which even the most subtle of paintings cannot render. They draw us into the poetic and sensuous world of gardens, which contemporary writers so tantalizingly describe: "for whereas every other pleasure commonly fills some one of our senses, this makes all our senses swimme with pleasure and that with infinite variety." The truth of William Lawson's words, from his *New Orchard and Garden,* 1618, is borne out to delicious perfection in needlework scenes, for example in a valance at Parham Park in Sussex. In this embroidery, a couple sit by their fountain, deep in amorous yet decorous dalliance. Around them nature—tamed yet exuberant—offers evidence of pleasure and beauty. Behind the couple a laden fruit tree gives them shade, and in the background a leafy trelliswork arcade invites to more private scenes. The gentleman raising an eloquent arm may be gesturing towards the fountain on his left to show the detail of the carving, but more likely he is declaring his love, for his other hand presses the lady's knee. And so the fountain scene is unperceived—by the gentleman at least—and only the spectator outside the embroidered story sees the cockerel at the lovers' feet, the gaudy peacock on the balustrade, the impudent rabbits among the knotted beds—what devastation do they reap? Only the spectator hears the embroidered fountain and wonders at the winged and naked cupid who directs the scene. Such moments of exquisite enjoyment would have been appreciated by the Elizabethans for their reality, and their transience.

Embroidery preserves these vanished pleasances, revealing the Elizabethan love of lively colours, scents and sounds. In these valances we may still enjoy the seclusion of intimate gardens and imagine the fragrance of the roses entwined so luxuriantly in the trelliswork. The scenes recall a sonnet by Bartholomew Griffin.

"See where my Love sits
in the beds of spices,
Beset all round with camphor,
myrrh and roses,
And interlaced with curious devices,
Which her from all the world
apart incloses.
There does she tune her lute
for her delight,
And with sweet music makes the
ground to move."

Carpenter's work was an essential feature in sixteenth century gardens, creating intimate enclosures where it was possible to see without being seen. Top: Alley and pavilion in carpenter's work. Bottom: Summer idyll in a valance from Parham Park. The alley in the background shows elaborate carpenter's work.

Music in gardens appears again and again as a theme in embroidery as if the transience of the one could be preserved in the other. Though embroidery lasts longer than the flowers it portrays, it too has an ephemeral quality, since the freshness of its colours may fade, fleeting like the sounds of music and the fragrance of flowers. In *Venus and Adonis* Shakespeare wrote:

"Fair flowers that are not gather'd
in their prime,
Rot and consume themselves
in little time."

and in *Sonnet V*:

"But Flowers distill'd though they
with winter meet,
Leese but their show, their substance
still lives sweet."

Elizabethan embroidery was part of summer's distillation, conserving the essence of the flowers, and the appearance of the garden at its zenith. In the French valance shown below, the knotted beds are bright with summer flowers and

under a rose arbour a table waits invitingly at the entrance to an alley in carpenter's work. This wooden framework covered in trellis and interwoven with plants was indispensable in Renaissance gardens, as it provided pleasant shade for walking in and for enjoying all the activities which came outside during the brief summer months when the garden was used as a decorative extension of the house. Its insubstantial and airy qualities were admirably suited to the lighthearted mood of the garden and open air entertainments. Books like Thomas Hill's *Gardeners Labyrinth* showed how it should be constructed. Using carpenter's work, amazing transformations could be achieved overnight and all manner of theatrical effects created. It is not surprising that Shakespeare set so many scenes in gardens of this kind where hidden meeting places abounded. This device is used in *Twelfth Night,* Act 2, scene 5, where the exuberant group led by Maria hide behind an arbour waiting for Malvolio to find their spurious letter purporting to be written by Olivia. In *Much Ado About Nothing,* Hero and Ursula walk up and down the alleys talking in loud voices knowing that Beatrice can overhear them from the bower.

"Where honeysuckles, ripened by the sun
Forbid the sun to enter!"

Act 3, scene 1

The Elizabethans perfected the art of living out of doors, making the most of warmth and sun—

"For never resting time leads summer on
To hideous winter, and confounds him there."

Shakespeare, *Sonnet V.*

Top: Juniper poles stand ready to complete a wall arbour with a table for outdoor meals. Woodcut from The Gardeners Labyrinth. *Bottom: A feast is set out in the shade of an alley in this detail from a French valance. "The herbers (arbours) erected in most gardens are to their much refreshing and delight."*

The deer and rabbits in the foreground of many Elizabethan embroidered furnishings illustrate the necessity for protecting the garden plants with a stout enclosure. Apparently innocent fountain figures were sometimes "full of concealed pipes which spurt upon all who come within reach."

With carpenter's work imitations of the long galleries and cabinets of the house could easily be created out in the fresh air. In place of hangings, the walls were decked with greenery, and the garden compartments came to resemble a series of rooms. Indoors and outdoors echoed each other. Inside, the galleries themselves would often be carved or painted, or hung with furnishings which imitated what was going on in the garden. In smaller gardens, carpenter's work was no more elaborate than the rustic bower or pergola of today, but in the gardens of the great, it reached levels of splendour and complexity reminiscent of fairy palaces. Some idea of its elaboration can be seen in the garden tapestries made in France and the Netherlands in the late sixteenth century. In these, as in the Franklin hanging, page 13, the garden is set within an idyllic landscape, but stands out from it through its sophistication and artifice.

The idea of gardens within a garden particularly appealed to the Elizabethans with their love of intricate effects and ingenious surprises. Trelliswork in particular was used to screen the view, allowing tempting glimpses into other parts of the garden. It added mystery to the scene, making one guess at what lay beyond, just as in fashionable dress, the lightest of gauzes or "cypress" veiled the gorgeous material beneath, or a network of slashes on sleeve or mantle only partly revealed a further layer of richly decorated stuff. The ornamental gardens generally lay on the far side of the house and fitted into a square or rectangular area. John Parkinson considered that "the foursquare form is the most usually accepted by all; being behind the house, all the best windows thereof opening onto it." A wide terrace lay below these windows, and steps led down to broad paths dividing the garden into various compartments. Each of the sections was complete in itself and separated from the next by a hedge or walk, or as in William Lawson's plan, shown opposite by a change of level. Here, six main sections on three levels are reached by a bridge across a little river. Two of the sections represent ornamental orchards, and the jaunty horse and his owner represent topiary work. "Your Gardiner can frame your lesser wood to the shape of men armed in the field, ready to give battell: or swift running greyhounds: or of well scented and true running Hounds, to chase the Deere, or hunt the Hare. This kinde of hunting shall not waste your corne, nor much your coyn."

The Tudor rose stands for the knot garden and both the "kitching" gardens were to be laid out decoratively with a neat arrangement of beds. Different views of the garden could be seen from the mounts sited at the four corners.

"In my opinion, I could highly recommend your orchard, if either through it or hard by it there should run a pleasant river with silver streams. You might sit in your Mount, and angle a peckled Trout, sleighty Eele, or some other dainty Fish." Lawson's garden springs to life in many of the embroidered scenes. In the Ashmolean valance, on page 23, the view corresponds to two of the sections of Lawson's plan, observed as if from the terrace where, in embroidered scenes, characters in the story meet together. Sir Henry Wotton, James I's ambassador to Venice, could have been describing this very garden when he wrote: "I have seen a Garden (for the manner perchance incomparable) into which the first Accesse was a high walke like a Terrace, from whence might bee taken a generall view of the whole Plott below but rather in a delightful confusion than with any plain distinction of the pieces. From this the Beholder descending many steps, was afterwards conveyed againe, by severall mountings and valings, to various entertainements of his scent, and sight: which I shall not neede to describe (for that were poeticall). Let me onely note this, that every one of these diversities was as if hee had beene Magically transported into a new Garden."

The "delightful confusion" was probably created by the variety of patterns in the knots and the miscellany of flowers planted in them. This effect must have particularly struck Sir Henry in contrast to the symmetrical designs in the gardens he would have seen in Italy where water, stone and greenery combined to make magnificent formal settings for villas and palaces and where flowers were relegated to a separate "secret garden." In Elizabethan England, flowers were given pride of place, grown not only in the knots, but in borders along the walls, and informally on grassy banks beside the streams.

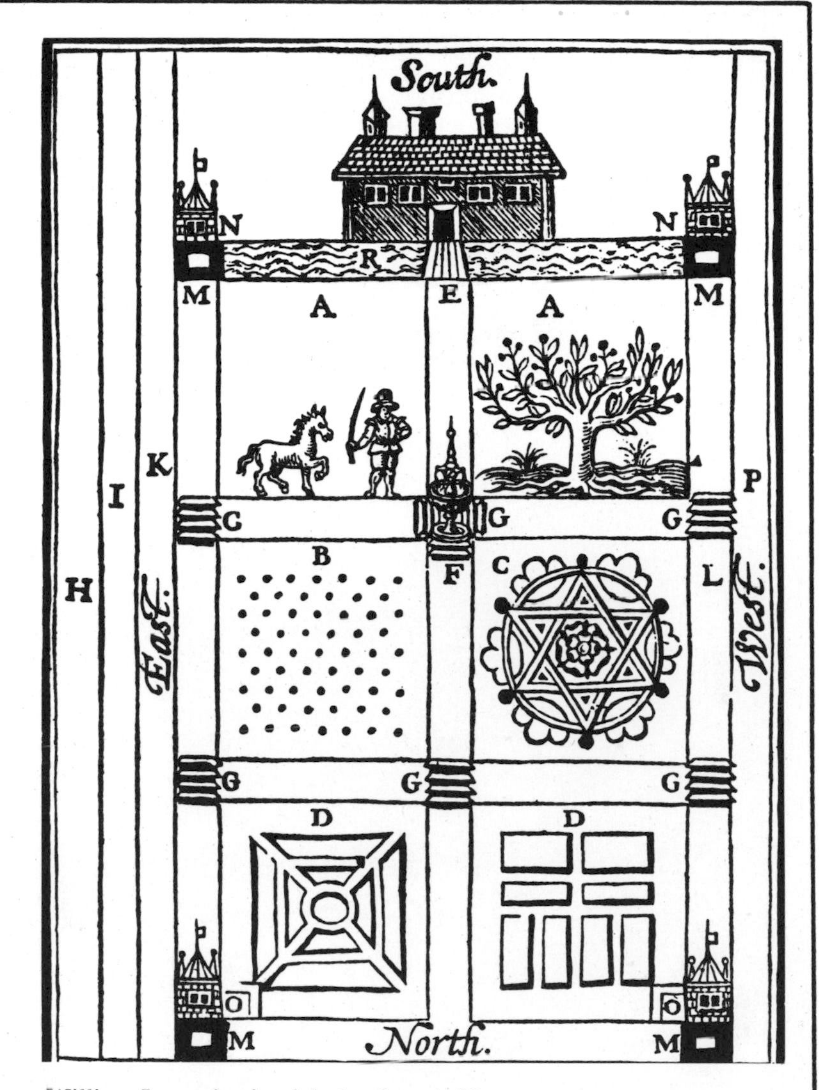

William Lawson's pictorial plan from A New Orchard and Garden *of 1618. The well-fenced garden has mounts and still-houses in each corner. "O" represents "good standing room for bees" in the "kitching gardens" which are also laid out ornamentally.*

AN INFINITE VARIETY OF SWEET SMELLING FLOWERS

Flowers also appealed for their virtues and properties, and all kinds of mysterious, magical and emblematic associations. For the Elizabethans it was as if, standing on the terrace overlooking the gardens they had before them not only, in Lawson's words, "an infinite variety of sweet smelling flowers decking with sundry colours the green mantle of the earth," but a living treasury ready to fill cosmetic boxes, medicine chests, still rooms and store cupboards.

Almost every plant had special, often mysterious or curative properties. William Turner, for example, in his *Newe Herball* of 1551 recommended spikes of lavender: "quilted in a cap and dayly worne they are good for all diseases of the head that do come of a cold cause and they comfort the braine very well." Not only caps, but gloves and other garments were delicately scented with perfumes made from the flowers whose likeness was embroidered upon them. John Parkinson noted this among the qualities of lavender: "the oyle for cold and benummed parts, and for to perfume linnen, apparrell, gloves etc. and the dryed flowers to comfort and dry up the moisture of a cold braine."

These beliefs affected all parts of gardening, from the choice of flowers and their almost magical properties to the growing and gathering of them. "Lyllies and Roses

planted together" for example "will both smell the pleasanter because of their amiable disposition" whereas the ranunculus is "of a very unsociable Nature and will not thrive mixed with or standing near any other sort." Well into the seventeenth century, farmers and gardeners in England were inclined to consider not merely the seasons and the weather when planting and sowing, but the phases of the moon. Thomas Hill, the writer of the first English gardening book, considered the moon's influence to be the most important factor.

Interest in plants increased with the developing science of botany, and collectors competed for varieties coming in from abroad. It was the "delectable variety" of the plants available that was shown off in the garden beds, set out individually as if in one of the new botanic gardens. The apparent confusion of mixed flowers was controlled and ordered by the dwarf evergreen borders outlining the beds. The borders and beds were themselves arranged within a regular framework so that the garden combined formal and informal elements in a blend particularly seductive to English taste.

Through most of the sixteenth century, these borders were in lavender, hyssop, thyme or rosemary. Box edgings, easier to maintain, but less pleasantly fragrant were a fashion brought in from Europe after 1600. The ordered profusion of this kind of arrangement has been recreated in the small enclosed knot garden at Cranborne Manor in Dorset, made only recently but in the true spirit of the originals. A most enticing collection of flowers is planted in each compartment, inviting the visitor to explore them more closely, and then drawing the attention from one part of the knot to the next. This enticement is paralleled in the embroidery that flourished on dress and furnishing.

Detail of an angler from the Bradford table carpet embroidered in tent stitch on linen canvas in the late sixteenth century. There were moats and streams in many sixteenth century gardens; fishponds with a jet of water flowing from pointed rocks became a favourite feature in seventeenth century needlework gardens.

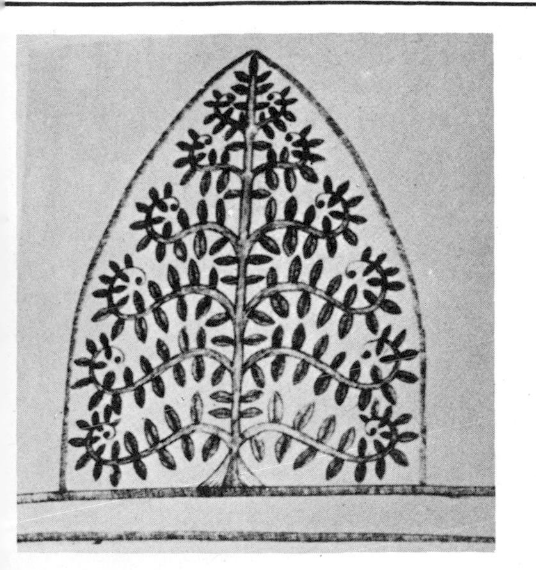

Above: Design for a nightcap by Thomas Trevelyon. Below: Two versions of the same allegory depicting a gentleman choosing between the Virtues. In the top valance a boy poses in the middle of a knotted maze as in the maze plans on page 34. The bottom valance shows how the garden settings as well as the characters were altered by different draughtsmen.

ROBES OF IMBROIDERED WORK

Embroidery was worked to cover the entire ground in intricate patterns, many of them small-scale replicas of the knots in the garden. The aptness of Gerard's comparison can be appreciated at once by comparing one of the knots in *A short instruction, very profitable and necessary for all that delight in Gardening* of 1592, with an embroidery pattern from Thomas Trevelyon's *Miscellany* of 1608, both based on a motif of interlacing hearts. Trevelyon knew all about knots for the garden, because he designed them himself and devoted a section to gardeners in a later collection of his designs. Only the curious tree roots and shoots round the edge of the garden pattern suggest that that is what it is. It would be perfectly possible to use it for embroidery. It would be no more difficult to work than the knot probably embroidered by Princess Elizabeth in 1544 as a bookcover for her stepmother, Catherine Parr. The knot was worked in silver thread and the corner spaces filled with four heartsease. These flowers may have been added for their emblematic

The Ashmolean Museum, Oxford

significance, or possibly as an afterthought because the spaces looked as if they needed filling. The crowded intensity of patterning and plants appealed equally to the taste of both embroiderer and gardener, and the opening verse of Thomas Campion's poem of 1601 applies to both their creations.

"And would you see my mistress' face
It is a flowery garden place
Where knots of beauties have such grace
That all is work and nowhere space."

The verse is charmingly illustrated by the portrait of Lettice Newdegate, shown on page 26, standing by a garden, the knot and interlacing patterns on the bodice of her dress echoed on a larger scale in the square beds of the knot garden behind her. Similar dense patterning covers Jane Bostocke's sampler shown on page 27, where formalised flowers, vines, strawberries and pomegranates framed in a diamond trellis of the most teasing complexity are set between interlaces and knots as intriguing to the eye as the "knots so enknotted it cannot be express't," that were one of the glories of Hampton Court palace.

The profusion of plants and patterns

The Bodleian Library, Oxford

Opposite: Elizabethan garden and embroidery designs of striking similarity. Interlacing hearts appear (top left) in the garden knot from A short instruction, very profitable and necessary for all that delight in Gardening, *in a pattern by Thomas Trevelyon from his* Miscellany *of 1608* (*top right*), *and in a red satin cushion worked in silver gilt threads* (*bottom*). *Above: Bookbinding for the* Mirror or Glasse of the Synneful Soul *embroidered by Princess Elizabeth for her stepmother Catherine Parr in 1544.*

contained within the orderly framework is like William Lawson's orchard. The simplicity of his pictorial plan is rather misleading, for when he writes about what the garden contains it is a cornucopia of fruit and flowers, the borders on every side "hanging and dropping with Feberries, Raspberries, Barberries, Currans . . . and Strawberries Red White and Green." In the beds were roses of every kind and "the violet nothing but the best for smelling sweetly . . . and all these by the skill of your gardener so comelily and orderly placed in your borders and squares and so intermingled that none looking thereon cannot but wonder to see what Nature corrected by Art can do."

Edmund Spencer in his poem *Muiopotmos* talks of the aim "t'excell the natural with made delights," and of the garden "with every herbe there set in order." With the Elizabethans these thoughts constantly recur. The art of the embroiderer who worked the red cushion, shown on page 24, with such perfection of technique and talent for design has transformed the flowers making them as decorative as jewels while at the same time managing to preserve their delicacy and fragility. Many of the best-loved flowers had been brought in from "the bank where the wild thyme blows, Where oxlip and the nodding violet grows", *Midsummer Night's Dream*, Act 2, scene 2. And from woodland and riverside came the strawberry Thomas Tusser describes:

"Wife unto thy garden and set me a plot
With strawberry rootes
of the best to be got;
Such growing abroade among
thornes in the wood

Collection of Mr Fitzroy Newdegate

Opposite: Detail from Jane Bostocke's sampler of 1598 crowded with intricate patterns including knots and interlaces like those decorating the bodice of Lettice Newdigate's dress seen left. The knotted bed in the garden beside her illustrates the aptness of John Gerard's comparison "of the earth aparelled with plants as with a robe of imbroidered work." In this type of knot, the pattern was outlined by plants such as rosemary, lavender, lavender cotton, germander, marjoram or thrift which were set close and carefully clipped. Box became more popular in the seventeenth century because it was less likely to gape and needed less frequent trimming. Above: A design from Gervase Markham's The Country Farm *suitable for this type of knot. In his opinion the interlacing threads of the pattern make the knot look as if it were made of "divers coloured ribands."*

Well chosen and picked
proove excellent good."

These flowers, tiny and unpretentious in their natural form, were taken up like so many jewels by the embroiderer who could "correct Nature" and exaggerate the decorative qualities of the plants making them more brilliant and "curious" to suit the age's taste for artifice and ambiguity. The silk and gold flowers' fascination lay in their being at once real and artificial. They were a reminder of the growing flowers in the garden and yet they were not the same.

A red velvet cushion is recorded in the inventory taken in 1601 of the furnishings belonging to the Countess of Shrewsbury, the redoubtable Bess of Hardwick. Silk roses are applied to the velvet, little sprigs set in the spaces of an interlacing strapwork pattern. The bold outline resembles not only a garden knot but the tracery in stone proudly crowning the roof line of the mansion and the patterns in plaster and marble in the rooms inside. The strapwork pattern on the cushion is applied in cloth of silver and the spaces are as curiously shaped as those in the knot patterns from William Lawson's *The Country Housewife's Garden*. The single sprigs within them are a reflection of the Elizabethans' interest in individual flowers and their pleasure in picking, wearing and arranging nosegays to "bewtifie and refresh the house," and strewing the floor with the clippings from the hedges in the knot gardens. Single sprigs and posies appear over and over again in Elizabethan portraits, held in the hand or pinned near the face beside their embroidered counterparts. They were chosen for their scent to override less pleasant smells and for their

beauty and significance to the wearer. John Gerard and the other herbalists always noted which flowers were best for picking. Gerard expresses his contemporaries' passion for flowers most tenderly when speaking of March violets in the garden which "have a great prerogative above others, not onely because the minde conceiveth a certaine pleasure and recreation by smelling and handling of those most odoriferous Flowers, but also for that very many by these Violets receive ornament and comely grace: for there bee made of them Garlands for the head, Nosegaies and posies, which are delightfull to looke on, and pleasant to smell to, speaking nothing of their appropriate vertues: yea Gardens themselves receive by these the greatest ornament of all, chiefest beautie and most gallant grace; and the recreation of the minde which is taken hereby, cannot be but very good and honest: for they admonish and stir up a man to that which is comely and honest; for floures through their beautie, variety of colour, and exquisite forme, doe bring to a liberall and gentlemanly minde, the remembrance of honestie, comeliness and all kinds of vertues."

Top: Mixed flowers are "so comelily and orderly placed in our borders and squares, that none looking thereon, cannot but wonder to see what Nature, corrected by Art, can do." Flower slips set out on a black velvet cushion. Bottom: Woodcut from Hill's The Gardeners Labyrinth. *Opposite: Queen Elizabeth at Wanstead House by Gheeraerts, c 1585. The arrangement of the flowers on her dress suggests how the garden beds were planted.*

Expecially popular were flowers like "Beares ears" (auriculas) which as, Parkinson wrote, "being many set together upon a stalke do seeme every one to be a Nosegay alone of itself."
Flowers were also arranged indoors to scent and brighten the rooms. A Dutchman, Livimus Lemnus, who visited England in the second half of the century found the effect charming: "Their chambers and parlours strewed over with fresh herbes refreshed mee; their nosegays finely intermingled with sundry sorts of fragraunt

Above: Long cushion cover recorded in the Hardwick inventory of 1601. The flower sprigs are placed like jewels in a silver setting. Left: Knot from William Lawson's The Country Housewife's Garden. *Outlined in silver leafed shrubs like santolina or lavender the knot would closely resemble "imbroidered work" in effect. Opposite: The flowers emblematic of France, England and Scotland framed in a twisting fret of plaited braid stitch on Mary Queen of Scot's cushion still glint with threads of silver and gold. The central emblem was taken from Gabriel Faerno's* Fables *of 1563 and bears the Queen's cipher. It shows frogs at a well, adding further cryptic meaning to the embroidery. The flowers and emblems are worked in silk in tent stitch, the background in cross stitch.*

flowers, in their bedchambers and privy rooms, with comfortable smell cheered me up, and entirely delighted all my senses."

If he had visited Hardwick, the Countess of Shrewsbury's last and most magnificent mansion, he would have been able to admire the fresh flowers' embroidered counterpart in almost every room, for Bess of Hardwick was not only one of the most ardent builders of the age, but also a great needlewoman. The cushions, table carpets and other furnishings are still there and their presence, even though they have lost their original freshness, still evokes the life and times of their creator in a unique and spellbinding manner.

Bess of Hardwick's interest in needlework made an immediate bond between her and her famous captive, Mary Queen of Scots. No record remains of the gardens of Hardwick in Bess's day, but at Holyrood Palace, Mary looked out over knots patterned with fleur de lys motifs. She may have been thinking of these when she embroidered a cushion with fleur de lys, roses and thistles, the emblems of France, England, and Scotland, linked yet confined by twisting threads of gold. All through her unhappy life, these flowers, the rose, the thistle, and the fleur de lys had come together, their political and personal, tragic and beautiful stems twining and interwoven. In her cushion, on page 31, these passionate preoccupations are given a decorative, yet eloquent setting. The poignancy of her thought is transformed—yet perpetuated.

The two noble ladies could call on professional help in drawing out their patterns, and part of the pleasure lay in searching the books in their possession for images to match all manner of personal allusions. When they had found what they wanted, the outline was marked on the canvas and then they worked the flowers, birds and animals, prettily shading them in tent stitch. They found many of the designs in emblem books, in the new

natural history books, where mythical animals were included among the real ones, and in herbals such as that of the Italian, Pietro Andrea Mattioli.
Often the small motifs were embroidered in tent stitch one at a time, and when enough of these "slips"—the same word was aptly used by gardeners to describe a cutting—had been completed, the embroiderer had the fun of moving them about on the rich ground to see how they looked best. This was certainly what happened in the hanging at Hardwick where people, animals, trees and flowers are assembled without any thought of scale. Much in the same manner, flowers growing between trees only slightly larger than themselves are arranged on the opening page of d'Aléchamps's *Herbal* of 1598. In the Hardwick hanging a lute player leans against an outsize plant while playing to a couple seated in an arbour of giant roses.
Only the great households kept professional pattern drawers in their employment. If she could not find a travelling draughtsman selling ready-drawn patterns, the embroiderer would prick round the woodcuts herself to transfer the flowers to her ground. Mary died a year after the publication of Jaques Le Moyne de Morgue's *La Clef des Champs* in 1586 so she cannot have used his enchanting book designed for those interested in painting, sculpture, goldwork, tapestry, and embroidery. The book is a collection of woodcuts, mostly of flowers and fruit, with a few birds and animals, providing exactly the simple, uncluttered yet decorative outline the embroiderer prefers. The tell-tale pricking of the copy in the British Museum speaks eloquently of the embroiderer's impatience to show off her skill in the working of such appealing motifs.
Le Moyne also painted exquisite water colours, which perfectly illustrate the delicacy, fragility and minuteness of the flowers which the embroiderer endeav-

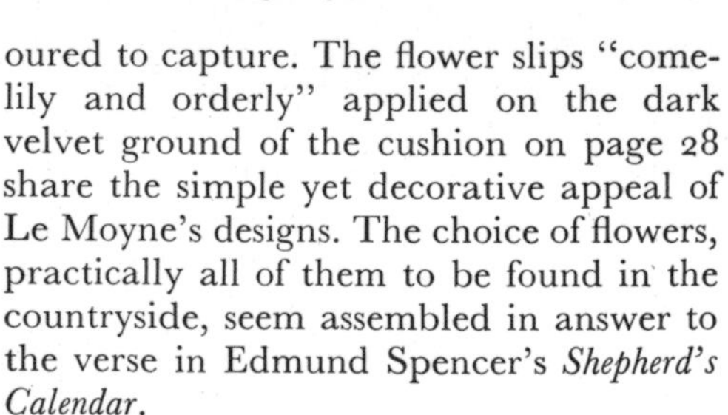

"The rose doth deserve the chiefest and most principall place among all flowres whatsoever." Above left: Watercolour of a rose from an album of exquisite studies of flowers and insects by Jacques Le Moyne de Morgues. Above: Briar rose in silk tent stitch on linen.
Left: Woodcut of a rose from La Clef des Champs. *Opposite above: Hanging at Hardwick with flower slips and other motifs including a rose arbour and musicians arranged regardless of scale. Below: Chapter heading from d'Aléchamp's* Herbal *of 1598. Embroiderers made use of the illustrations in contemporary herbals where the same peculiarities of scale were to be found.*

oured to capture. The flower slips "comelily and orderly" applied on the dark velvet ground of the cushion on page 28 share the simple yet decorative appeal of Le Moyne's designs. The choice of flowers, practically all of them to be found in the countryside, seem assembled in answer to the verse in Edmund Spencer's *Shepherd's Calendar*.

"Bring hether the pinke
and Purple Cullambine
With gelliflowers,
Bring Coronations, and Sops in wine,
Worne of Paramoures;
Strowe me the ground with
Daffadowndillies
And cowslips and Kingcups and loved
Lillies . . ."

The miscellany of insects amid the flowers on the cushion evokes the same poet's *Muiopotmos,* in which a butterfly flutters happily into a garden where:

"Lavish nature, in her best attire
Powres forth sweete odours
and alluring sights;
And arte, with her contending,
doth aspire
T'excell the naturall with made
delights;
And all, that faire or pleasant
may be found,
In riotous excesse doth there abound.

There he arriving round about doth flie,
From bed to bed, from one to
other border,

CAVENDO TVTVS
FVIMVS

Above: Detail of the gardens at the Château of Gaillon from du Cerceau's Les Plus excellents Bastiments de France *of 1576. The rectangular beds behind the magnificent garden pavilion and fountain are filled with patterns as complex and varied as those in the leaves of the pillow cover (opposite). The mazes are identical to those illustrated (right) from Thomas Hill's book,* The Profitable Art of Gardening, *which was published in 1568.*

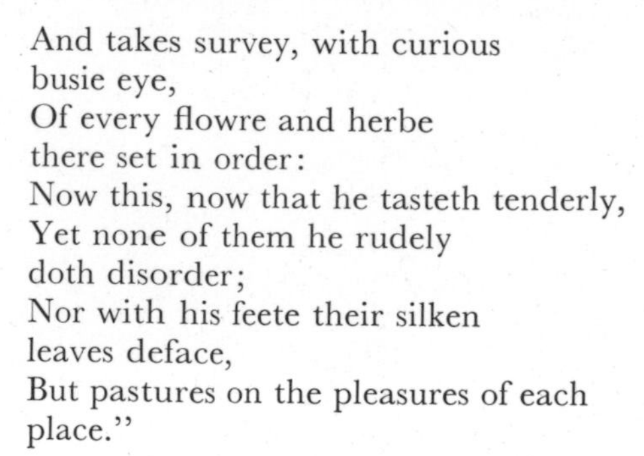

And takes survey, with curious
busie eye,
Of every flowre and herbe
there set in order:
Now this, now that he tasteth tenderly,
Yet none of them he rudely
doth disorder;
Nor with his feete their silken
leaves deface,
But pastures on the pleasures of each
place."

"T'excell the naturall with made delights" was exactly the intention of the Elizabethan ladies each with "curious busie eye," as they made complex patterns and messages, composed of every "herbe there set in order," and though the ladies, famous or unknown, are dead and gone, like the flowers they observed, we may still enjoy the "silken leaves."

KNOTS AND MAZES

The little beds in Hill's *The Gardeners Labyrinth* show the effect of the knots at their least elaborate with just a simple edging. When flowers were used in the knots they were said to be "open" but when the patterns became a "riotous excesse" of interwoven bands, there was no room for flowers and then the knots were "closed". Such was the maze, as perplexing and complex as the convolutions of blackwork.

Complexity like "delectable variety" was greatly admired by the Elizabethans whether in speech, dress or decoration. While the lord of the manor set out to amuse and confuse his guests with a maze "to sport in at times," his wife puzzled out the path of the thread in mazes of cutwork and lacis or in the labyrinthine intricacies

of blackwork.

Simplified mazes appear in many embroidered garden scenes, and the draughtsman who put the boy in the centre of the maze in the Ashmolean valance on page 23 may have been familiar with the plans in Thomas Hill's *The Profitable Art of Gardening* with figures standing in the middle. Almost identical mazes to the ones in Hill's book were the central feature in the layout at the Château of Gaillon in the 1570's. This garden was almost as famous in the sixteenth century as Versailles was to become in the seventeenth. The beds at Gaillon, each with its individual intricacy, are held together in the foursquare walled enclosure of the complete garden, so that the owner may look into the whole area to see the beds and to watch his guests as they admire the knots or puzzle out their path within the low hedges of the maze; this intricacy is echoed in the squares of delicate cutwork, each different and each intriguing, which were assembled into the elaborate unity of the fashionable ruffs.

Hill recommends his maze to be laid out with "isope and tyme, or with winter savery and tyme. For these do well endure all winter through greene." The pleasing monochrome effect of these intricate designs reappears in blackwork, where complex patterns engage and intrigue the spectator leading him on to explore the twists and turns of the path and all that they conceal or reveal, like the hero in Du Bartas' *Divine Weeks* published in 1584.

"Musing, anon through crooked walks
he wanders,
Round-winding rings,
and intricate meanders,
False guiding paths,
doubtful beguiling strays,
And right-wrong errors
of an end-less Maze."

Blackwork was either worked in tiny geometric patterns on the counted thread of the background fabric, or in a speckling technique where minute stitches resemble the shading of an engraving. Coiling patterns, so favoured by embroiderers and repeatedly used well into the seventeenth century have the feeling of an "endless maze" spreading all over the surface of the material as you would expect in a textile design, although in the pillow cover shown above, the border controls the "delightful confusion" and "delectable variety" within with neatly alternating leaves and grapes. In the cover the embroiderer has produced a *tour de force* of invention and ingenuity in which the twisting stems of the vine lead to different parts of the design, where each leaf encloses a new pattern, and visual surprises abound. Once again "all is work and nowhere space."

STUART GARDENS

There is no excellent beauty that hath not some strangeness in the proportion

Francis Bacon, Essays XLIII, "Of Beauty", 1625

FLORAES PARADISE

The gardens and embroidery of the early seventeenth century became increasingly elaborate. This was the age of the prodigy houses with their splendid gardens; noblemen like Lord Burghley had great plant collections, and the new exotics from abroad were eagerly cultivated. Jacobean gardens like the one at Hatfield House in Hertfordshire built in 1611 for Robert Cecil, Lord Burghley's son were laid out with more compartments, more fountains and complex waterworks while the dress of the courtiers glittered with a profusion of gold and silver threads, ribbons and spangled rosettes which were as intricately frilled as the most cunningly cultivated double roses or gillyflowers.

Court masques and theatrical and ingeniously contrived effects delighted the Jacobeans just as much as they had the Elizabethans. "Fantasticall conceits" to amuse both host and guest at such revels were described by Sir Hugh Plat in *Floraes Paradise*, which first appeared in 1608. How often were his instructions for making "flowers candied as they grow" actually carried out? On a hot summer morning, as soon as the dew was dry, balm, sage or borage were moistened with a mixture of gum and rosewater and then sprinkled with fine sugar from a specially made box "holding a paper under each flower to receive the sugar that falleth by, and in three hours it will candie or harden upon; and so you may bid your friends after dinner to a growing banquet." Alternatively, the host could intrigue his guests with "flowers and leaves gilded and growing" contrived in the same way but covered with leaf gold instead of sugar. They would remain "a long time faire notwithstanding the violence of the rain."

Such sparkling and festive conceits would have been the perfect decorative complement to the costume of those taking part in the entertainments. The dress of both ladies and gentlemen was embroidered on sumptuous silk, satin and velvet grounds with a dazzling array of small flowers, leaves, birds, insects, and other devices worked in bright silks and brilliant metal threads which must have glittered as deliciously as the crystallized confections of *Floraes Paradise*. Furnishings were equally gorgeous, and contemporary inventories read like a cross between a jeweller's and a plantsman's catalogue. At the time of his death in 1614 the Earl of Northampton

Opposite: Ladies working at their embroidery in a garden from an entry in the Album *of Gervasius Fabricius of Salzburg in 1613. The garden flowers in the vase might suggest colours and stitches to the embroiderer but her designs were most likely to be drawn from books. Early seventeenth century gardens kept the fountains, knots and carpenter's work of the previous age.*

Opposite: Portrait of Margaret Laton c 1610. The glittering embroidery on the jacket is as fancifully conceived as a banquet of growing flowers. Roses, honeysuckle and pinks spring from a single coiling stem as if from a magical plant inhabited by vivid parrots, butterflies and snails. The gaiety and sparkle of the bespangled blooms contrasts with the crisp white geometry of the ruff echoing the garden contrast of bright flowers and cool shimmering water made to play in canopies from the fountain jets. Right: Unworked panel of white satin marked out with a design of an arbour entwined with multi-flowering plants. Similar designs were worked both in stumpwork and canvaswork. Above: Canvaswork panel of an arbour trained with grapes, roses and tulips. The simultaneous appearance of sun, moon, rainbow and clouds heighten the effect of a wonderland.

owned the following pillow covers: "A paire wrought with beastes and flowers silke and golde. Another paire embroidered with waterlilly leaves, kinges fishers and other birds and flowers silk and gold. Another paire embroidered with a runninge worke of pomgranets, grapes and roses silke and golde. A paire embroidered with roses and other flowers in colours silke and gold. Another paire with a traile worke of sundrie flowers, strawberyes and pinckes."

The trailing and coiling patterns of blackwork were also worked in coloured silks and silver gilt thread, as they had been in the previous century, and they enlivened furnishings and dress with ever more fanciful and charming decoration. The many different blooms apparently growing from a single stem were echoed in the real arbours and alleys of the garden where plants were still carefully trained on trelliswork—as shown in the illustration on page 40 from Gervase Markham's *The Country Farm.* The plants would soon mingle and interweave to create the illusion of a single, many-flowered plant just as they did in embroidery. "You shall set white thorne, eglantine and sweet briar mixt together and as they shall shoot and grow up so

shall you wind and pleach them within the lattice work making them grow and cover the same." Vines, peas and red-flowered beans were set amongst the climbing flowers, and they too can be seen in the coiling stems of needlework.

The Needle's Excellency was a popular pattern book printed by James Boler in 1634. On the title page, Industry exemplifies the pleasure and profit of embroidery in a garden with pots set out on small square beds and flowers interwoven on the trellis fence. The designs for cutwork embroidery given in *The Needle's Excellency* are as intricate as the garden knots in contemporary manuals. But the embroiderer, inspired by John Taylor's introductory poem, might well be eager to vary her subjects:

> "The needle's work hath
> still bin in regard,
> For it doth art, so like to nature frame,
> As if it were her sister, or the same.
> Flowers, plants and fishes, beasts, birds,
> flyes, and bees,
> Hills, dales, plaines, pastures, skies,
> seas, rivers, trees;
> There's nothing neere at hand,
> or farthest sought,
> But with the needle may be shap'd
> and wrought."

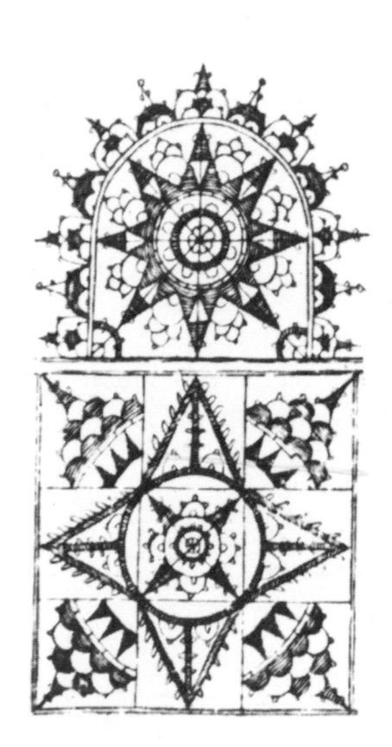

Sadly, cutwork patterns were no help with the naturalistic rendering of "flowers, plants and fishes" and if the embroiderer were to realize John Taylor's suggestions, designs and hints would have to be found elsewhere—for example in Richard Shorleyker's *A Schole-house for the Needle*, published in 1624, where there were "sundry sorts of spots (motifs) as Flowers, Birds and Fishes," which would enable the embroiderer to "compose many faire workes." She could set out the simple but spirited motifs in all manner of decorative combinations "according to her skill and understanding." In the latter half of the century, there were many more motifs to

Below: Trelliswork fence from Gervase Markham's The Country Farm *of 1613. As the plants grew up they would cover the framework and eventually be clipped into three-dimensional topiary shapes along the top. The topiary at Hampton Court included "all manner of shapes, men and women, sirens, French lilies and delicate Crenellations." Opposite above: Plants trained on a simple trellis fence on the title page of Johann Siebmacher's* Newes Modelbuch *of 1604. Below: Three decades later the same title page and many of the patterns were used by John Boler in* The Needle's Excellency. *It is interesting that the garden and the figure of Industry remain unchanged whereas the dress of Wisdom and Folly have been updated, suggesting that fashions in gardens and embroidery change more slowly than in some other arts like dress.*

choose from. The London print-sellers sold sheets of patterns, either singly or in collections with titles similar to Shorleyker's. One was Peter Stent's *Booke of Flowers Fruits Beastes Birds and Flies*, published in 1650. There were also picture books of the most popular Bible stories and sheets depicting allegorical and royal characters. The pictures and motifs were adapted by professional pattern drawers or by the embroiderer to create scenes often set in endearingly childlike gardens in which the same flowers and features constantly reappear. These elements were to be found in real gardens, an indication that the embroiderer was influenced by the illustrations and information in garden books and by the gardens she herself enjoyed.

The best-loved garden book of the seventeenth century was John Parkinson's *Paradisi in Sole Paradisus Terrestris, A Garden of all Sorts of Pleasant Flowers*, published in 1629 and dedicated to Queen Henrietta Maria. The title page shows Adam grafting an apple tree in the Garden of Eden. The apple tree is no

PARADISI IN SOLE
Paradisus Terrestris.
or
A Garden of all sorts of pleasant flowers which our English ayre will permitt to be noursed vp:
with
A Kitchen garden of all manner of herbes, rootes, & fruites, for meate or sause vsed with vs,
and
An Orchard of all sorte of fruitbearing Trees and shrubbes fit for our Land
together
With the right orderinge planting & preseruing of them and their vses & vertues
Collected by John Parkinson
Apothecary of London
1629

Qui veut parangonner l'artifice a Nature,
Et nos parcs a l'Eden, indiscret il mesure.

Le pas de l'elephant par le pas du ciron,
Et de l'Aigle le vol par cil du mouscheron,

Opposite: Title page from Parkinson's Paradisi in Sole Paradisus Terrestris *of 1629. "Outlandish" flowers dwarf the human figure. The Scythian lamb feeds by the river. Right: Bookbinding containing the Book of Common Prayer and the Holy Bible printed in 1607. Silver-threaded rivers running out of Eden pass under a group of patterned rocks, the scale is as curious as on Parkinson's title page.*

The Metropolitan Museum of Art, Gift of Irwin Untermeyer, 1964

bigger than the nearby lily, and Adam himself looks tiny compared to the luxuriant carnation beside him. These discrepancies of scale, even more surprising in some of the printed sheets of patterns, recur in embroidery throughout the century. The Garden of Eden appealed strongly as a fanciful and decorative theme which enabled the embroiderer to assemble all manner of weird and wonderful animals, fish, and insects amongst the marvellous plants described in such books as Parkinson's. Versions of the theme were worked using various methods on all sorts of different articles: book bindings, pillow covers, and pictures which were an innovation unthought of in Elizabethan times when all embroidered articles were intended to be used.

Despite advances in the sciences, old superstitions and beliefs still lingered on in seventeenth century minds, and the borderline between fact and fiction was often confused. On Parkinson's title page, there is the figure of an animal hanging limply on a stem or small trunk which grows out of the ground. This is the "Scythian lamb," a creature reported in imaginative descriptions of the Far East, which was said to burst from a bud on the plant and wither away when it had eaten the foliage around it. This naive and fantastic tale was devised to explain the white woolly heads of the cotton plant, which had not yet been introduced to the West; and though it was unlikely to exist in reality, the picture intrigued the imagination, like the mermaids and other strange creatures in the pools of the embroidered gardens.

Parkinson described his book as "a Garden of all Sorts of Pleasant Flowers which our English Ayre will Permitt to be noursed up", and the tenderness with which he describes his plants suggests that he thought of them as children needing his constant affection and attention. John Rea expressed much the same idea in his *Flora* of 1665. "Love was the Inventer, and is still the Maintainer, of every noble Science. It is chiefly that which hath made my Flowers and Trees to flourish, though planted in a barren Desart, and hath brought me to the knowledge I now have in Plants and Planting: for indeed it is impossible for any man to have any considerable Collection of noble Plants to prosper, unless he love them: for neither the goodness of the Soil, nor the advantages of the Situation, will do it, without the Master's affection; it is that which animates, and renders them strong and vigorous; without which they will languish and decay through neglect, and soon cease to do him service."

The response was summed up by Parkinson when he referred to his book as a "speaking Garden where the many herbs and flowers with their fragrant sweet smells do comfort and as it were revive the spirits." It was not enough to admire the flowers, the real enthusiast had to procure

them and look after them himself.
"Anemones are so full of variety and so dainty that the sight of them doth enforce an earnest longing desire in the minde of anyone to be a possessour of some of them at least." The stylized pansies worked in the beaded panel shown opposite, express the embroiderer's affection for the flowers she has chosen, and her pleasure in preserving them. Embroidery, like gardening, is a time-consuming activity demanding patience and perseverance. The keen plantsman's "earnest longing desire" to possess certain plants also inspires the embroiderer, making her work strong and vigorous.

OUTLANDISH FLOWERS

Parkinson distinguished between "English" flowers, like pansies, and "Outlandish" ones like tulips: "our age being more delighted in the search, curiosity and rarities of these pleasant delights than any age I think before." He described how tulips should be planted "one colour answering and setting off another that the place where they stand may resemble a peece of curious needlework . . ."
Tulipomania in England never reached the same heights as in Holland, but the "wonderful variety and mixture of colours" and their "stately and delightfull forme" made tulips among the most costly and highly prized of all "outlandish" flowers to be treated as "so many jewels". On Parkinson's title page the outlandish flowers, mainly bulbs, far outnumber the English ones. It is easy to see how collectors, gardeners and embroiderers must all have been excited by such wonderful novelties—who could tell what rare properties, strange shapes and wondrous sizes might yet appear? The ever widening range of colours was described more accurately and poetically than today —tulips could combine tones of gredeline

The Metropolitan Museum of Art, Gift of Irwin Untermeyer, 1964

(pale grey), quoist (the colour of a dove's breast) and gilvus (a very pale red).
In Crispin de Passe's *A Garden of Flowers* published in 1615, a gentleman leans on the balustrade of a garden which has hardly changed since the last century, except in the variety of exotic plants in the beds. This choice collection includes a display of tulips, hyacinths, iris, crocus, a yucca and, in the place of honour, a crown imperial. In 1615 many of these plants were newly introduced to Europe. The crown imperial which grew wild in Persia had been sent to Vienna by the botanist de l'Ecluse in 1576, and the crocus had been sent to Gerard from Paris by Jean Robin. Robin was the director of Henri IV's gardens at the Louvre, and it was this appointment that brought him in contact with the King's embroiderer, Pierre Vallet. Vallet created the embroidery designs which were worked by Marie de Medici and the ladies of her court. He was always looking for new subjects and based many of his designs on the plants he found in Robin's own garden which was full of novelties and was often visited by Queen Marie herself. Robin began to grow rare flowers especially for Vallet to engrave as motifs for embroidery. The king became patron of their project and in 1608 the finest blooms of all were assembled in a book entitled *Le Jardin du Roi Henry IV* which was dedicated, in the most eloquent and extravagant terms, to the Queen. Although intended as a pattern book, the exquisite flowers were engraved naturalistically, making them less useful for the embroiderer than those in the latter part of Crispin de Passe's *A Garden of Flowers* where the plants have been simplified in outline. Though his book was originally intended for colouring, these outlines have always appealed to the embroiderer. The flower sprigs and clusters of nuts and fruit were transformed into miniature trees set on hillocks inhabited by birds, insects and imaginary plants which add to the decorative and fanciful effect of the plates.
In the early seventeenth century, the native flowers of Elizabethan embroidery were joined by "outlandish" newcomers, some real and some imaginary. These mysterious and multi-flowering plants appeared on sweet bags and other embroideries. Though they seem merely to be figments of the embroiderer's imagination, such amazing creations were also the ambition of every gardener interested in

Opposite above: The Garden of Eden, late sixteenth century panel in applied work. God stands at the centre, the expulsion of Adam and Eve is on the right. "When God had made man after his own Image he placed him in Paradise. What was Paradise? But a Garden and Orchard of trees and herbs, full of all pleasure and nothing there but delights," William Lawson. Opposite below: The Fall. Detail from early seventeenth century pillow cover. Below: Beaded panel of pansies dated 1657, "Naturs flowers soon doe fade ful long we last cause art us made."

the secrets of grafting. Whole books with titles like *The Fruiterers Secrets,* or *Cornucopia, a Miscellaneum of Lucriferous and Most Fructiferous Experiments* were written, full of strange theories and experiments for grafting different fruit on a single plant.

THE PLEASANT DELIGHTS OF A CURIOUS ORCHARD

Ladies perusing Sir Hugh Plat's book *Floraes Paradise* for "Secrets in the ordering of Trees and Plants" might have paused when they read his suggestion for "grafting plummes on a willow to come without stones," and imagined how fanciful and decorative the effect of such a strange hybrid might be in embroidery.

In his *Description of England* written at the end of the sixteenth century, William Harrison had admired the skill of gardeners who were "not only excellent in grafting the natural fruits, but also in their artificial mixtures whereby one tree brings forth sundry fruits, and one the same fruit of divers colours and tastes, dallying as it were with nature in her course, as if her whole trade were perfectly known to them."

Some embroidered trees bore a variety of fruit as if the gardener's dreams had at last come true. The wonderful crops are reminiscent of Andrew Marvell's poem describing the pleasures of his garden.

"What wond'rous life is this I lead!
Ripe Apples drop about my head;
The luscious clusters of the vine
Upon my mouth do crush their Wine;
The Nectarine and curious Peach,
Into my hands themselves do reach;
Stumbling on Melons, as I pass
Insnar'd with Flow'rs, I fall on Grass."

The seventeenth century orchard was exceptionally well stocked with a rich variety of fruit trees and bushes, and was designed to be as decorative as the pleasure garden, set out with paths, arbours and fountains. The flower season which had not yet been extended by plant introductions from China and Japan was much shorter than today, and the orchard was doubly appreciated for its beauty in autumn. Vineyards and orchards were among the "Flowers, Starres and Paradises of the Earth" for Ralph Austen, who described their delights in *A Treatise of Fruit Trees* in 1653, echoing Gerard's comparison with "robes of imbroidered work": "Is it not a pleasant sight to behold a

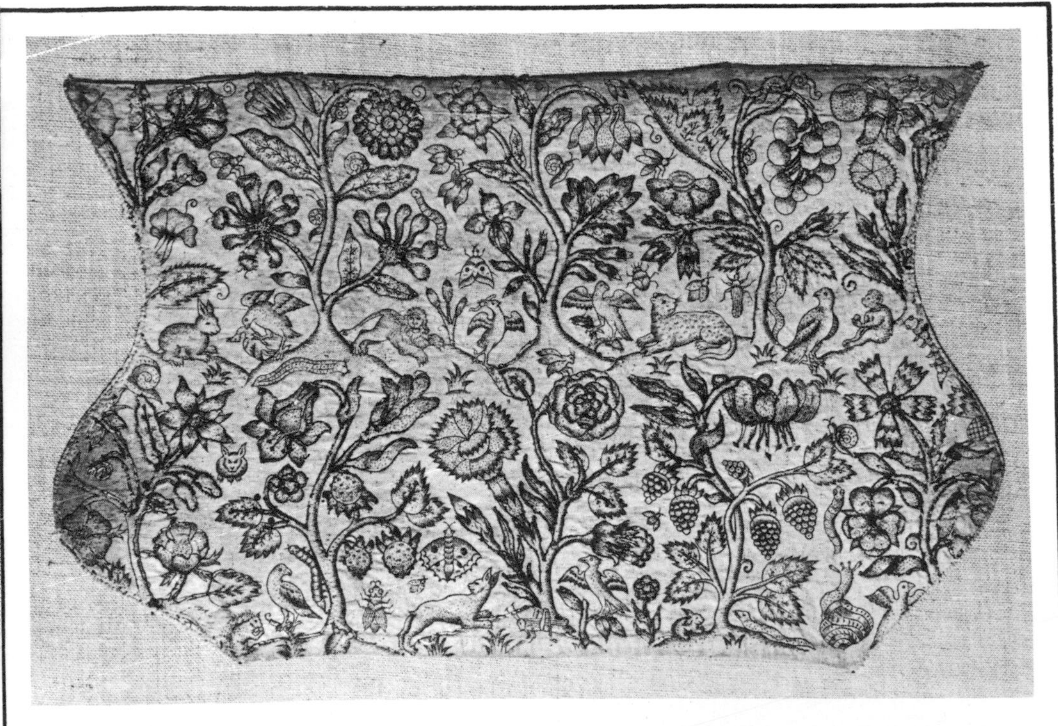

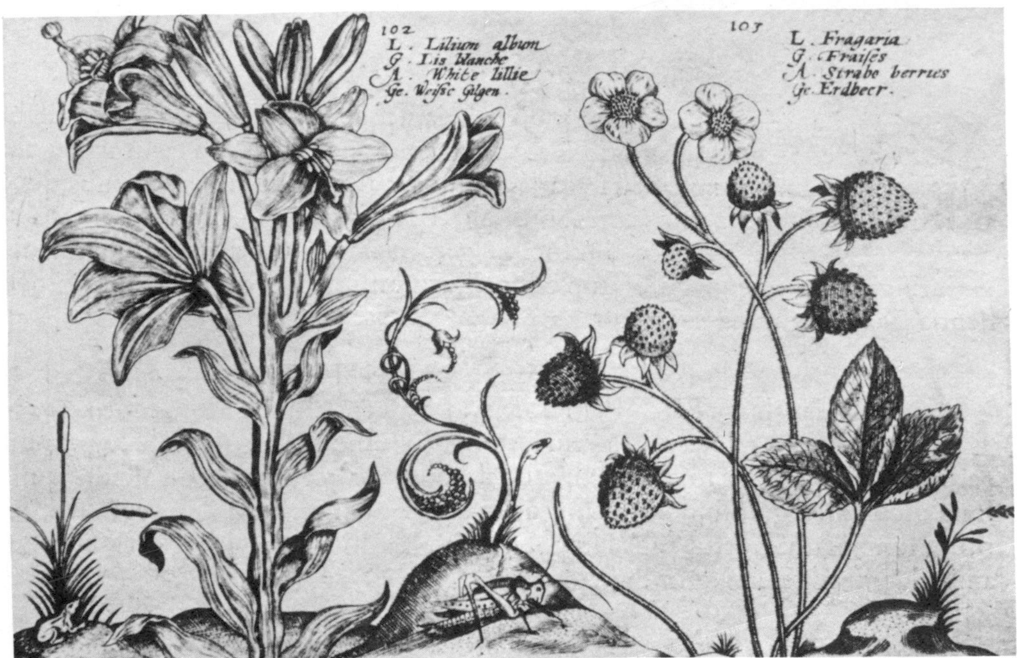

multitude of Trees round about, in decent forme and order, bespangled, and gorgeously apparelled with green Leaves, Bloomes and goodly Fruits, as with a rich Robe of imbroidered work, or as hanging with some precious and costly Jewels or Pearles, the Boughs laden, and burdened bowing downe to you, and freely offering their ripe fruits, as a large satisfaction of all your labours."

The orchard was a cornucopia for all the senses, and garden writers like William

Opposite: The spring garden from A Garden of Flowers *by Crispin de Passe. "And now the Florists fly about to see the chief pleasure of gardens." Many of the new plant introductions can be seen in the beds. Top: Jacobean coif printed and partly worked with a design in blackwork. Fanciful trees grow on diminutive hills with small creatures on every side. Bottom: Similar effects in an engraving from the last section of* A Garden of Flowers. *The grasshopper is typical of de Passe's affectionate and witty treatment of his subjects.*

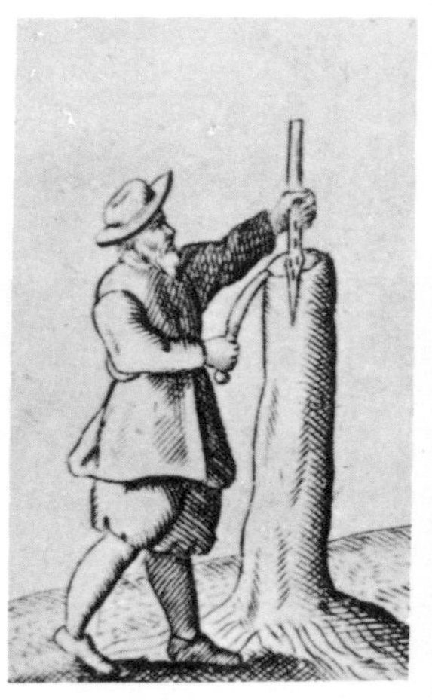

The Metropolitan Museum of Art, Gift of Irwin Untermeyer, 1964

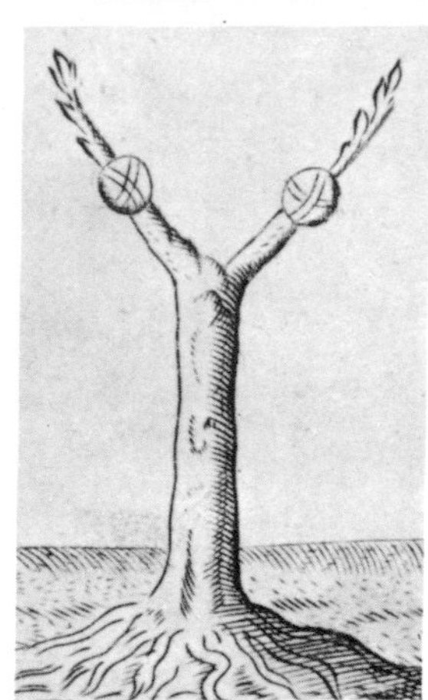

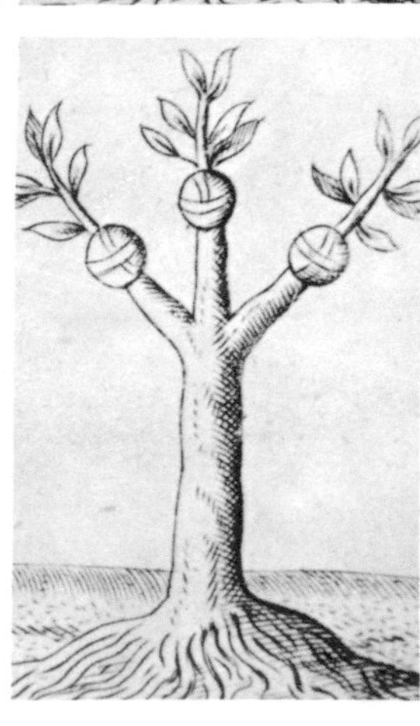

Coles in *The Art of Simpling* in 1652 described the visual enchantments, the taste of the fruits, the fragrant smells, and even the feel of the plants "some as soft as silke and some as prickly as an Hedgehog . . . The eares have their recreation by the pleasant noise of warbling notes, which the chaunting birds accent forth among the murmuring leaves."

The numerous birds worked in the embroidery of the period are an indication of the seventeenth century gardener's affection for them. William Lawson thought "one chief grace that adorns an orchard" was "a brood of Nightingales," which were not only charming company, but would "help you cleanse your trees of caterpillars and all noysome worms and flyes. The gentle Robbin-red-breast will helpe her . . .", and "if you have ripe Cherryes or Berries" you would be sure of the company of blackbirds and throstles which "sing loudly in a May morning." (*A New Orchard and Garden*, 1618).

Fruit trees were colourful and decorative, and the embroiderer, attracted by their luscious crops, often exaggerated the size of the fruit on the trees. But was her work quite as fanciful as it appears? Trees on which several varieties of fruit are grafted are commonplace now and so are dwarfing stocks which make picking the fruit a far less tedious business, as well as fitting into smaller gardens. In the seventeenth cen-

Opposite above: Picture of a fruiting tree, animals and birds embroidered in silks in the first half of the seventeenth century. The variety of fruits on the tree recalls the contemporary craze for grafting described by Abraham Cowley in The Garden.

"He bids th'ill natured crab produce
The gentler apples' winy juice.
He doth the savage hawthorne teach,
To bear the Medlar and the Peach."

Opposite below and far left: Grafting practices and fishpond from The Expert Gardener. *Above: Title page of* A Treatise of Fruit Trees *by Ralph Austen.*

tury dwarf trees were already a reality clearly described in *Floraes Paradise.* "If you would have an orchard of dwarfe trees, suffering none to grow above a yard high . . . nippe off all the green buds when they first come forth, which you find in the top of the tree, with your fingers." These miniature orchards were illustrated in garden books and may have provided inspiration for the embroiderer.

CABINETS OF CURIOSITY

The passionate interest of the age in the exotic, the curious, the strange and the merely odd are reflected in the craze for stumpwork which decorates the cabinet shown on page 50, and in that real cabinet of curiosities, known as Tradescant's Ark. This was set up in their garden at Lambeth by John Tradescant and his son, two of the greatest gardeners, explorers and collectors of the age. The ark contained the weirdest miscellany of objects: "Two Feathers of the Phoenix tayle. Elephants head and tayle only. Flea chains of silver and gold," to name a few. It was all part of the current taste for collecting together and admiring quite unconnected items, which were esteemed for their "curiosity." The embroiderer was following this collecting fashion in putting together oddly assorted motifs, and applying minute shells, pearls, pieces of mica and chips of glinting minerals to create wonderfully strange effects in stumpwork.

Stumpwork was originally known as

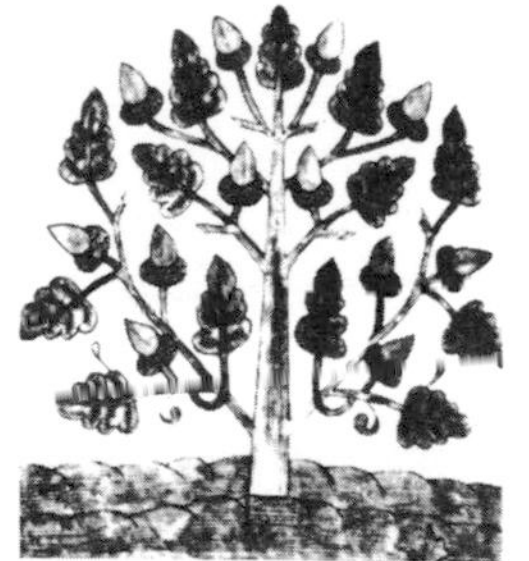

raised work—a more accurate description of the three-dimensional effects achieved by padding and applying detached motifs. It was in fashion from about 1650 to 1680 when it was popular with young girls from the affluent homes of Stuart England who worked it in panels for pictures, mirror frames and cabinets. A large number of these survive, some of the cabinets embellished with a tiny garden or a bed of flowers on the lid. The flowers were often worked in detached buttonhole stitch within flexible wire frames so that they stood up realistically and were entirely three-dimensional. Once completed, the embroidered panels were usually sent away to be made up professionally into cabinets, these were often lined and padded with pink silk and contained silver-topped bottles and many little drawers.

Everything about the cabinets must have delighted the girls who made them, especially if they had first had the long and taxing exercise of working one, if not two, long samplers. When starting on a cabinet there was the fun of choosing the biblical or mythological story and characters to ornament it, for the embroidery was pictorial, and the panels at the sides and on top neatly divided the story into different episodes. Whether the various panels were marked out by a professional, or by the embroiderer herself, the gleaming ivory satin which had recently become available to the embroiderer and which formed the ground for most stumpwork, was an invitation to start using a wealth of silks, metal threads, beads, pearls and even peacock feathers. The stitchery showed off the meticulous technique she had learned while working her sampler, and the inventiveness which she was now at liberty to display. It is tempting to imagine that John Rea, the author of *Flora* had these cabinets in mind when he wrote in 1665: "We will proceed to the Flower-Garden, and fashion it in the form of a cabinet with several boxes fit to receive and securely keep Natures choicest jewels." Parkinson, too, had thought of his flowers as precious jewels, and Rea intended his book to describe the new plants which had arrived since Parkinson's day. Again, it was the variety of plants that appealed to him. "A choice collection of living beauties, rare plants, flowers and fruit" were "indeed the wealth, glory and delight of the garden" and "the most absolute indication of the owner's ingenuity, whose skill and care is chiefly required in their choice culture and position."

The embroiderer chose her flowers and worked them with care and skill. She placed them in a wonderland setting quite unlike the detailed replicas of real gardens depicted in Elizabethan work, though still peopled by a similar cast of biblical and allegorical characters now dressed to resemble Charles I or Charles II and their Queens, in laces and periwigs instead of ruffs and farthingales.

By the middle of the century, fashions in great gardens were beginning to reflect the influence of the new French formal gardens—grander, yet simpler and more unified. But English flower lovers continued either to give their flowers a little plot by themselves, or like Rea in 1665, to persevere with a "complex fret" of 23 "divisions outlined with white painted rails" for his collection of flowers. Rea emphatically rejected the open and plainer style of the French garden, which he called an "immured nothing." He preferred the "essential ornaments, the verdant carpets of many pretty plants and pleasing flowers" with which even a green meadow was "spontaneously embroidered." The frontispiece of John Worlidge's *Systema Horticulturae* of 1677 depicts the plain grass plots of a fashionable new garden, but his text shows a continuing delight in gardens made for the sake of flowers. "Scarce an Ingenious Citizen that by his confinement to a Shop, being denied the privilege of having a real Garden, but hath his boxes, pots or other receptacles for Flowers, Plants, etc. In imitation of it, what curious Representations of Banquets of Fruits, Flower pots, Gardens and such like are painted to the life to please the Eyes and satisfye the fancy of such that either cannot obtain the Felicity of enjoying them in reality, or to supply the defect that Winter annually brings?"

The "curious representations of flowers and gardens" whether in canvaswork, flat silk stitchery, or raised work on satin, have real and interesting links with contemporary garden literature and with features in actual gardens. The trees reflect popular grafting practices and the flowers echo the gardeners' ambition to make blooms as vivid and showy as possible. This was expressed in William Harrison's *Description of England* in the 1570's: "for so cunning and curious are our gardeners now in these days that they presume to do what they list with Nature, as if they were her superiors."

The "cunning and curious" fingers of the needlewoman had gradually begun to make flower petals and butterflies' wings lift off the surface of the material until they were completely detached, while fruit and snail shells began to swell realistically. Fine wire and padding were concealed with stitchery in the making of the inhabitants and background in this novel three-dimensional world.

Opposite: Stumpwork cabinet which opens to reveal a miniature orchard of tiny trees arranged at the corners of two square plots. Two more plots represent the flower garden. Episodes from the story of Abraham ornament the sides. Below: Stumpwork picture illustrating the story of David and Bathsheba. The flowers and fruit on the arch above the fountain are three-dimensional.

VERDANT SCULPTURE

The amusement provided by stumpwork —both in the doing and the beholding— has an affinity with the pleasures of topiary which continued in vogue until the end of the century, when the stumpwork craze was at its height. Barnaby Googe had

recommended, in *Four Books of Husbandry* published in 1577, that rosemary could be "sette by women for their pleasure to growe in sundry proportions as in the fashion of a Cart, a Peacock, or such like things as they fancie." But Parkinson preferred yew: "it is so apt that no other can be like unto it, to be cut, lead and drawn into what forme one will, either of beasts, birds or men."

The little figures along the top of Markham's hedge, shown on page 40, designed to be shaped into topiary when the plants grew up, would not have appealed to Lord Bacon, who had pronounced views on garden decoration. He did not like "images cut out in juniper or other garden stuff: they be for children," though paradoxically he did like the idea of having fruit grown into moulds so "you may have apples in the form of pears or lemons. You may also have fruit in more accurate figures of men, beasts or birds, according as you make the moulds." If your hostess had been reading Gervase Markham's *English Housewife*, you might

Collection of David Tron

Opposite: Panel for a mirror frame. Many of the motifs were worked separately and then applied to the satin. Top: A mid-seventeenth century picture with an elephant and other animals and fruit in raised work. Huge flowers stand on small, carefully shaded hillocks. Bottom: Detail from a late sixteenth century tent stitch valance of a menagerie garden. The couple in the curious house look out over their moat where a "strange spotted beast" stands on an island. This animal's greenish colour differs from the more naturalistic tones used for the elephant, camel and others suggesting that it might be made in topiary.

find salads with carrots cut into fantastic shapes of birds and beasts.

The strange shapes and peculiar discrepancies of scale, the "mixum gatherum" of people and decorative motifs create a similar friendly atmosphere in both topiary and seventeenth century stumpwork gardens. The quaint but charming company assembled on the embroiderer's ground were matched in the real garden by the verdant shapes of dogs, lions, bulls, fishes, and fowl, which could be made by covering frames with greenery as suggested by Sir Hugh Plat in the 1675 edition of *The Garden of Eden*.

Topiary had its detractors, however. In his essay on "Verdant Sculpture" published in *The Guardian* in 1713, Alexander Pope attacked the excesses of the topiary fashion, which had continued well into the eighteenth century. The curious contents of his "Catalogue of Greens" included:

"Adam and Eve in Yew, Adam a little shattered by the fall of the Tree of Knowledge in the great storm: Eve and the serpent very flourishing.

The Tower of Babel, not finished.

St. George in box: his arm scarce long enough, but will be in condition to stick the dragon by next April.

A green dragon of the same, with a tail of ground-ivy for the present. N.B. These two not to be sold separately.

Edward the Black Prince in cypress.
A Laurustine bear in blossom, with a juniper hunter in berries.
A pair of giants, stunted, to be sold cheap.
A Queen Elizabeth in phylyrea, a little inclining to the green sickness but of full growth. [Phylyrea should be Phillyrea—the jasmine-box or mock-privet].
An old maid of honour in wormwood.
A topping Ben Jonson in laurel.
Divers modern poets in bays, somewhat blighted, to be disposed of a pennyworth.
A quickset hog, shot up into a porcupine, by being forgot a week in rainy weather.
A lavender pig, with sage growing in his belly.
Noah's ark in holly, standing on the mount, the ribs a little damaged for want of water."

SHADES OF ALICE

Although Lord Bacon considered topiary childish, some of the garden features he did approve of sound just as quaint as those to be found in seventeenth century needlework. His imaginary garden was to be laid out formally on thirty acres of ground with a succession of flowers for every month. The main garden was not to be "too busy or full of work." Bacon was ahead of his time when he insisted that there should be plenty of "grass kept finely shorn." Knots aroused the same displeasure as topiary: "they be but toys: you may see as good sights many times in tarts." A third of the garden forming the heath was to be "framed as much as may be to a natural wildness." Here there were to be "little heaps in the nature of mole hills (such as are in wild heaths); to be set some with wild thyme; some with pinks; some with germander; some with strawberries . . . Part of which heaps to be standards of little bushes pricked upon their top. The standards to be juniper; holly; berberries . . . redcurrants, gooseberries." Lord Bacon's essays were so well known that the embroiderer was quite likely to have read them, and she would have been all too familiar with the random trails of real mole hills in the garden. Embroidered people, buildings, flowers and animals were often set on small mounds or among undulating hillocks receding gently into the background, both of which acted as useful devices for isolating one incident or character from another.
Thus in the many versions of the story of David and Bathsheba, Bathsheba holds the centre of the stage as she bathes in an elaborate fountain, while the other characters act out their part of the story, each on a separate grassy mound. David spies Bathsheba from the roof of his toy castle, summons Uriah the Hittite and sends him to his death; past, present and future all meet within the embroidery. Stories in which women were the heroines, inspiring either admiration or pity, were particularly popular with the embroiderer. Abraham, banishing the servant girl Hagar and her little son Ishmael were repeatedly chosen as the central group in embroideries based on a series of engravings illustrating the Bible story, all put together under a sunlit sky with the episodes occupying individual hillocks.
In one such scene a very tall lily stands between Abraham and Hagar rather like the scene in *Alice through the Looking Glass* when Alice endeavoured to climb the hill in order to see the garden. She wandered up and down corkscrew paths until finally

Above: Purse and matching pincushion. Roses and pansies grow on the same plant embroidered in coloured silks and silver thread. The work is exquisitely finished with plaited drawstrings and tassels. Such purses often contained presents either of money, sweets or perfume. Opposite above: David spying on Bathsheba bathing at a fountain pool. Picture in tent stitch c 1655. Opposite below: A large lily and caterpillar are among the disproportionate motifs on a book cushion.

she came to a large flower bed. "'O Tiger Lily!' said Alice, addressing herself to one that was waving gracefully about in the wind, 'I *wish* you could talk!' 'We *can* talk,' said the Tiger Lily, 'when there's anybody worth talking to.'"

The scale and atmosphere in seventeenth century embroidery make such a conversation seem quite possible. "Into your garden you can walk, And with each plant and flower talk," suggested John Rea in *Flora*, and although seventeenth century embroiderers could not enjoy Lewis Carroll's fantasies, they might have come across Ralph Austen's *Dialogue, or familiar discourse betweene the Husbandman and Fruit Trees* published in 1676. The husbandman walking in an orchard asks the fruit trees if they really can talk. They reply "we can speak all languages . . . according as people please to discourse with us, so do we answer them: every man in his own language." The husbandman settles for English and compliments them on their appearance. "Me thinks ye swagger, and are very brave this May morning; in your beautifull blossomes and green leaves whence have yee all this gallantrie?" The fruit trees, unlike Alice's impudent flowers, are pious, prim, and disconsolate—they answer: "Many people . . . come from time to time to walk among us and look upon us and commend us for brave and handsome trees . . . but never speak a word to us."

Opposite: The trees and people on a similar scale in this raised work picture evoke the talking trees in Ralph Austen's Dialogue. *Dwarf trees were common in many seventeenth century orchards. Below: Detail of a butterfly in silks on linen, early seventeenth century.*

In the needlework scenes of the period the tops of the trees are on just the right level to speak to the people around them; and indeed, the peculiarities of scale put plants, people, animals and insects all on the same footing. In these embroideries the bizarre is translated into visual terms, capturing the atmosphere of strangeness so apparent in the poetry of Andrew Marvell. In the poem *Upon Appleton House*

"Men like Grasshoppers appear
But grasshoppers are Gyants there."

Flowers stand as stiffly to attention as those in embroidery:

"See how the Flowres as at Parade
Under their colours stand displaid:
Each regiment in order grows,
That of the Tulip, Pink and Rose."

Marvell's poetry is full of garden images. In *The Garden* he describes a knot laid out as an elaborate sundial:

"How well the skilful Gardner drew
Of flow'rs and herbes this Dial new;
Where from above the milder Sun
Does through a fragrant Zodiack run;
And, as it works, th'industrious Bee
Computes its time as well as we.
How could such sweet
and wholesome Hours
Be reckon's but with herbs and flow'rs."

The bee is like Spencer's butterfly on page 32, and the quantity of insects in Elizabethan and Stuart embroidery reflects both the scientific interest and the affection they inspired at the time—especially bees, which like plants had virtues and properties. "Bees are kept throughout the world for the delicate

The Metropolitan Museum of Art, Gift of Irwin Untermeyer, 1964

Food, pleasant Drink and wholesome Physick they yield" and "their curious architecture is to be admired." The diarist John Evelyn had a transparent beehive given him by the "most obliging and universally curious Dr Wilkins" of Wadham College, Oxford, who had transparent apiaries "built like castles and palaces," so he could study the habits of the bees. Entire books were written about them—one, *The Feminine Monarchie* written by Charles Butler in 1623, even included a bees' madrigal with the notes hummed by the Queen and her workers written out in staves. The embroidered insects match these rather fey notions to perfection, for the tiny creatures seem to have personalities of their own, like the intimate and friendly flowers, animals and people around them.

There were beehives in Elizabethan and Stuart gardens, and at the beginning of the seventeenth century, the growing of mulberry trees for silk worms was encouraged by James I. The charming winged creatures in contemporary needlework were chosen primarily because they were delightfully decorative, but they are also a reminder of a time when bees, butterflies and other insects in gardens were far more numerous and varied than they are today.

Above: The five Senses and the four Elements. "Hearing" plays in an arbour by the rocky fountain and miniature galleon in "Water's" pool. Opposite: Joke fountains were favourite garden features, more amusing for hosts than for guests. Above: Bathsheba at the pool. The expression on the fountain figure's faces suggests humorous possibilities like those illustrated in (below) Worlidge's Systema Horticulturae.

SILVER FOUNTAINS

"Roses have thorns
and silver fountains mud,
Clouds and eclipses
stain both moon and sun,
And loathsome canker lies in
sweetest bud." (*Sonnet XXXI*)—

whereas in the embroidered garden the smiling sun always shines, the flowers are in full bloom and the fountains and pools are clear and glittering. The same scene was repeated over and over again, whether the heroine was Bathsheba, or Susannah glimpsed by the Elders hiding in an arbour, or Hagar or Rebecca at their respective wells. For the embroiderer, pools, fountains and grottoes were as much an opportunity for a virtuoso performance as they were in real gardens, so popular that they were included in the scene whether they were part of the story or not. Shapes, colours and textures were combined and

contrasted using all the varied stitches and materials at the embroiderer's command. The water could be patterned horizontally and the rocks vertically, and tiny spirals of purl (coils of silk-covered wire), beads and spangles glinted among them just as the minerals did in the real and much-loved grottoes of the time.

At Enstone in Oxfordshire there was a famous grotto which had been built around a real rock as jagged and curious in outline as any devised by the embroiderer. The rock was enclosed in a building and was the central feature in a spectacular water display mounted for guests after they had banqueted in the upper room. Here the ceiling repeated the watery theme with paintings of Susanna and the Elders, and Hagar finding the well. The rock and the room around it concealed a network of pipes controlled by cocks to produce spellbinding effects. A great jet of water tossed up a silver ball and arcs of falling water seen through the sunlight created an artifical rainbow.

These ingenious waterworks originally

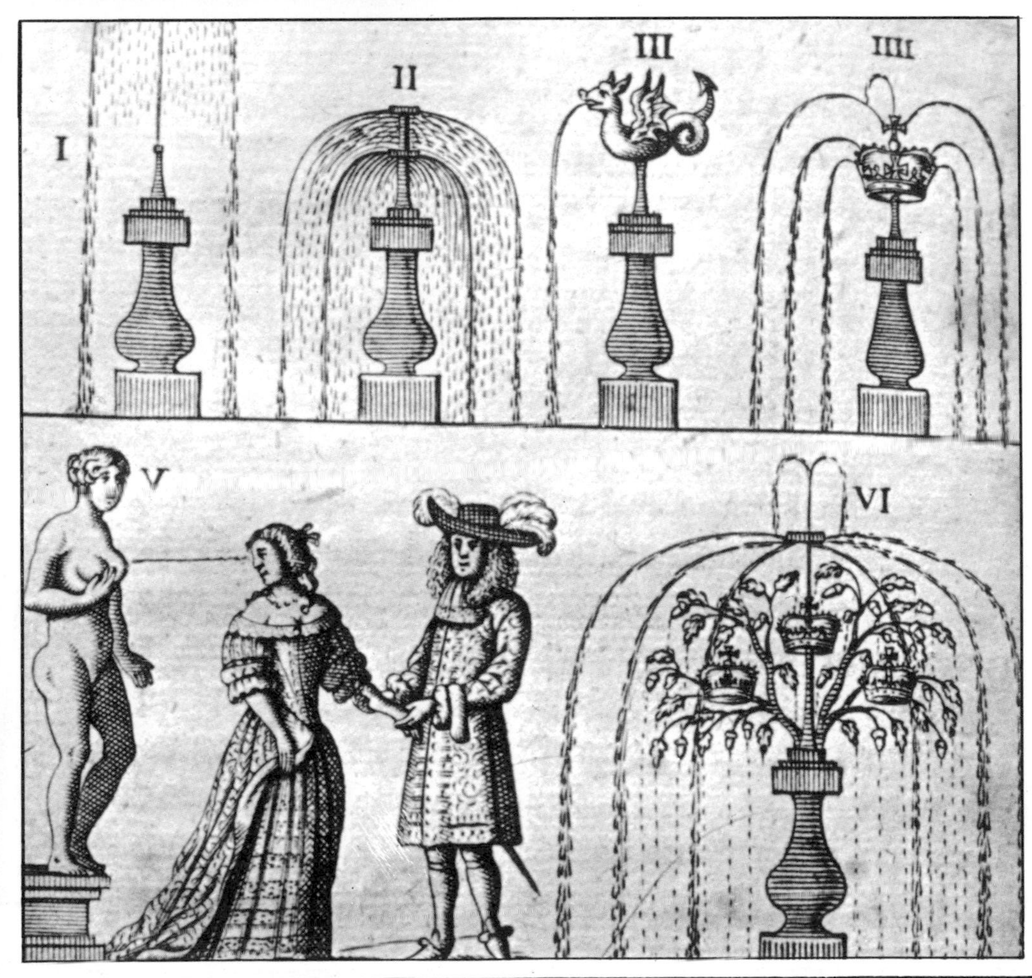

came from the gardens of Renaissance Italy and gave many visitors a "thorough wetting" when they were installed in great English gardens like Hampton Court, Theobalds and Whitehall. In John Worlidge's book *Systema Horticulturae* the illustration of various fountains is equally humorous and lighthearted, and his remarks on grottoes seem as appropriate for the embroiderer as for the gardener. "It is a place that is capable of giving you so much pleasure and delight that you may bestow not undeservedly what cost you please on it, by paving it with marble or immuring it with stone or Rockwork, either naturally or resembling the excellencies of Nature."

Fountains were often set in fishponds, which were both ornamental and useful. In August of 1685, John Evelyn visited Lady Clarendon's house at Swallowfield in Berkshire where he admired the "delicious and rarest fruits" in the orchard, the fine trees, shrubs and flowers. "My lady being so extraordinarily skill'd in the flowery part, and my lord in diligence of planting . . . but above all, the canall and fish ponds, fed by a quick and swift river, so well and plentifully stor'd with fish that for pike, carp, breame and tench, I never saw anything approaching it." Over thirty years before, Evelyn had made his own triangular fish pond with an "artificial rock" next to the "little retiring place" he built in the meadow at Wotton in Surrey. There are plans for triangular fish ponds in Gervase Markham's *A Way to Get Wealth* published in 1638. There were special mounts above the ponds where one might enjoy the sight of the fish which "show to the sun their wav'd coats dropt with gold." This description, from Milton's *Paradise Lost*, seems equally apt to describe the embroidered fish leaping in the rocky pools beneath the gold-rayed sun. Their bodies gleamed with metal threads and pieces of purl, waved and chequered with tiny patterns ingeniously worked out to contrast with the stitchery of the water and the plumage of the birds who float among them—ducks, swans and brilliant kingfishers invariably with a fish in their beaks.

The embroiderer's fanciful creations may also have resembled the artificial fish ornamenting the bed of the stream at Hatfield. Set among gorgeous shells and mysterious rocks, they were made lifelike by the reflections of the water pouring into the stream from an extraordinary marble basin dominated by a statue of Neptune standing on painted artificial rocks. Even closer to the artifice of the needlework ponds and rocks was Francis Bacon's water garden at Gorhambury where there was a lake with flowery islands presided over by statues of nymphs and tritons. Round the lake there were gilt images and "glasses coloured for the eye" and the bottom of the lake was covered with pebbles of several colours which were "worked into various figures such as fish". In the imaginary garden of his essay, Bacon recommended similar glittering effects. The surface of the pond or pool was to be "embellished with coloured glass and such things of lustre." The two types of fountain he described can both be seen in contemporary embroidered gardens: "the one, that sprinkleth or spouteth water; the other a fair receipt of water of some thirty or forty foot square but without fish or

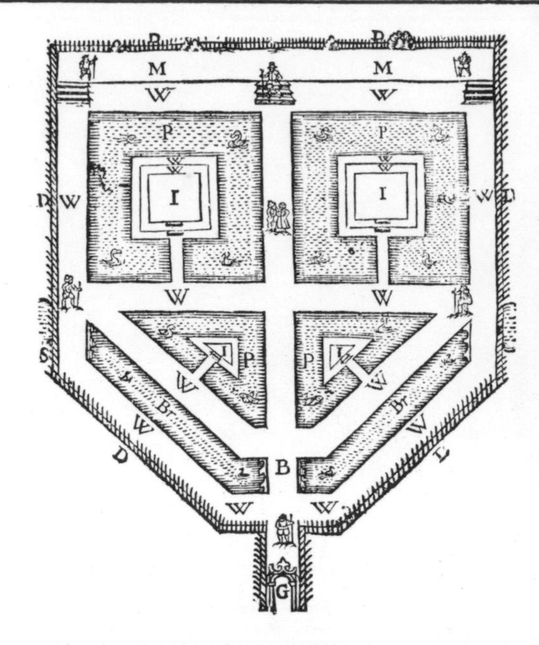

Above: "A platform for ponds," a plan for laying out triangular fish ponds from Gervase Markham's A Way to Get Wealth *published in 1638. The walks between the canals and ponds were to be ornamentally planted with fruit trees and willows and mounts were to be set up in the corners. There was a similar water garden at Theobalds where "with a boat one may have much pleasure and row among the shrubs." Opposite: Picture in raised work with a fountain pool. Small pools in seventeenth century gardens were designed for fishing, bathing and keeping water birds. At the end of the century more extensive canals and basins were in fashion.*

slime or mud." The second kind "which we may call a bathing pool" is reduced to the dimensions of a plunging pool by the embroiderer. Such pools did also exist—like the one at Packwood House in Warwickshire still complete with its brick walls, just as they appear in embroidered scenes. At Hatfield, Robert Cecil, Lord Burghley's son, employed French experts to create the wonderful water garden and John Tradescant his gardener, supplied the shells for the stream. The garden contained 24 figures of golden lions—harking back to Cardinal Wolsey's day, when the pond garden at Hampton Court was crowded with scores of carved and gilded "heraldic" beasts. These creatures were also seen in the knots and topiary: "made all of herbs with dulcet sweetnes."

In the seventeenth century there were real menageries and aviaries where rare animals and birds were on view. James I had established a menagerie in St James' Park which was much enlarged by Charles II who introduced the famous pelicans and the improbable figure of a crane with a wooden leg.

Wild beasts were a part of the embroidered gardens too. Lions with manes as meticulously curled and waved as a gentleman's periwig sit smiling on grassy hummocks and in cavernous grottoes, or stand twirling their tails opposite spotted leopards, both equally disinterested in the docile unicorns, stags, and camels on the surrounding slopes. The embroiderer chose these wild and mythical animals to inhabit the garden from the patterns available in books. And whether she was aware of it or not, she was following a tradition that goes back to the menageries attached to royal palaces, like the one at Woodstock in Oxfordshire where Henry I kept "lyons, leopards, strange spotted beasts, porcupines, camells and such like animals."

THE GRAND MANNER

Neatness and elegancy

Joseph Addison

PARTERRES OF EMBROIDERY

The French formal garden was known to many Englishmen by the middle of the seventeenth century. In his diary, Samuel Pepys wrote on 22 July, 1666 ". . . walked to Whitehall . . . discoursing of the present fashion of gardens to make them plain." Simple geometric grass plots had replaced the medley of plants in the knots, their smooth surface echoing the lustrous plain silks from which all trace of the previous rich and fanciful embroidery of flowers, fruit, insects and birds had disappeared.

The change to the French formal style was seen also in the introduction of the parterre, and the decline and gradual disappearance of the knot. The pleasant variety of flowers and patterns in the knot gardens had no place in the spacious unified designs in the French style where the beds were laid out symmetrically with their patterns matching as perfectly as those on a gentleman's coat.

This was exactly how the effect was described by George London and Henry Wise, who were the foremost nurserymen and designers in the reigns of William and Mary, and Queen Ann. In *The Retir'd Gardener,* published in 1710, London wrote: "Before I proceed to speak further of Parterres it will be requisite for the information of the Reader to explain what I mean by Imbroidery, cut-work and Turfs, or green Plots. Imbroidery is those Draughts which represent in Effect those we have on our Cloaths, and that look like foliage, and these Sorts of Figures in Gardener's language are called *Branch-work*. Below this certain Flowers seem to be drawn which is that part of the Imbroidery which we call *Flourishings*."

Patterns for knots continued to appear in garden books well into the second half of the seventeenth century but by then they were gradually being replaced in fashionable gardens by parterres in the new style introduced from France by Charles II. The transition was described in Sir Thomas Hanmer's *Garden Book* of 1653. "The whole designs or laying out of garden grounds are much different from what our fathers used. In these days the borders are not hedged about with privet, rosemary or other such herbs which hide the view and prospect . . . all is now commonly near the house laid open and exposed to the sight of the rooms and chambers, and the knots and borders are upheld only with very low coloured boards or stone, or tile.

'Neither is there a Noble or pleasant Seat in England but hath its Gardens for pleasure and delight." John Worlidge illustrates the latest fashion in Systema Horticulturae. *Plain turf plots showing off the excellence of English grass replace the flowery knots. Pepys suggested that flowers should be grown in "a little plot by themselves," out of sight from the main garden.*

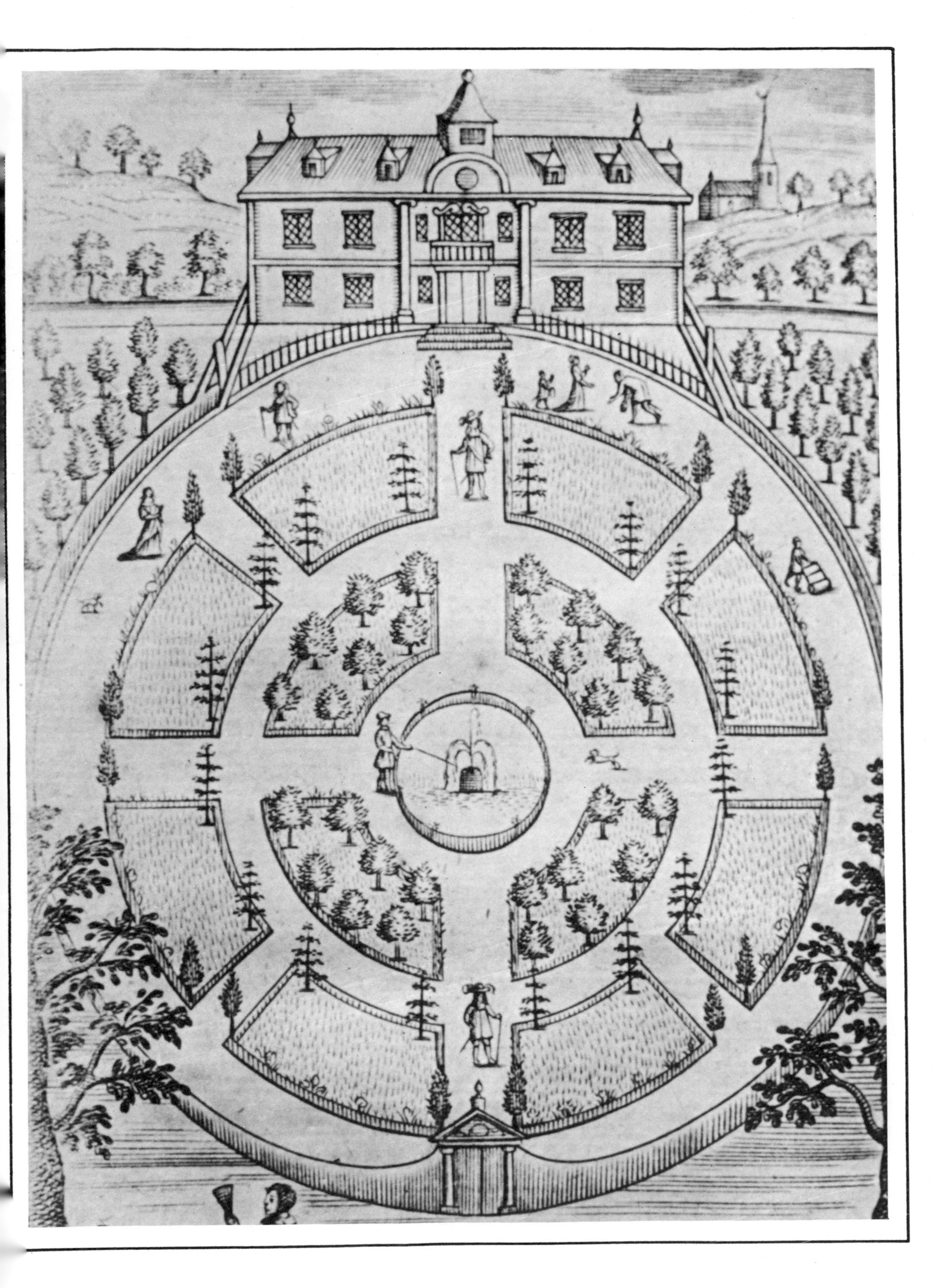

If the ground be spacious, the next adjacent quarters or parterres, as the French call them, are often of fine turf, but as low as any green to bowl on; cut out curiously into embroidery of flowers and shapes of arabesques, animals or birds, or feuillages (leaf shapes), and the small alleys or intervals filled with several coloured sands and dust with much art, with but few flowers in such knots, and those only such as grow very low, lest they spoil the beauty of the embroidery.

"Those remote from habitation are compartments, as they call them, which are knots also, and borders destined for flowers, yet sometimes intermixed with grasswork, and on the outside beautified with vases on pedestals, or dwarf cypresses, firs, and other greens which will endure our winters, set uniformly at reasonable distances from each other, and in these great grounds beyond are either labyrinths with hedges cut to a man's height, or thickets for birds cut through with gravely walks, or you have variety of alleys set with elms, limes, abeles, firs and pines, with fountains cascades and statues. All florists have, besides the embroidery and compartments where their guests amuse themselves, a little private seminary, to keep such treasures as are not to be exposed to every one's view . . ."

The use of the word "embroidery" as a gardening term is far more explicit than the poetic comparisons of Gerard and Ralph Austen's "robes of imbroidered work."

The term "parterre de broderie" was first used at the beginning of the seventeenth century when Charles Mollet laid out the gardens at Blois and Fontainebleau for Henri IV, and the embroidered parterre

The Metropolitan Museum of Art, Gift of Irwin Untermeyer, 1964

Below: Late seventeenth century music party in a garden uninfluenced by changing fashions. The beds full of flowers below the terrace balustrade are reminiscent of the scene in Crispin de Passe's spring garden on page 46. Peacocks, one can be seen in the background, had been popular in gardens since the previous century. Opposite above right: Esther before Ahasuerus, engraving from Historia Sacrae Veteris et Novi Testamenti *c 1660. Below: Canvaswork picture based on the engraving but altered to include a garden scene. Above left: Plain grass parterre from Worlidge's* Systema Horticulturae *whose layout is similar to the garden in the embroidered picture.*

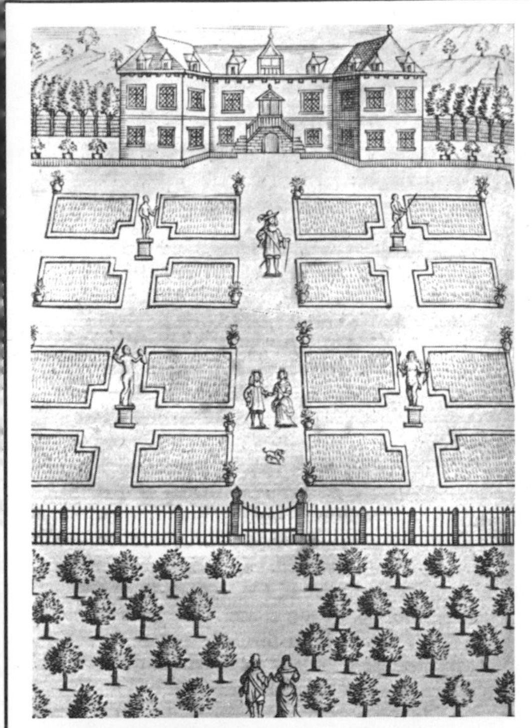

Page 66: Detail from an early eighteenth century picture. A palm tree adds a "whimsical air of novelty" to the pastoral scene. Page 67: "The Management of the Flower Garden in particular is oftentimes the Diversion of the Ladies." Charles Evelyn, The Lady's Recreation, *1718. Lady gardener with a watering can, embroidered in simple flat stitches on silk. Above: "Rural Landskip," early eighteenth century canvaswork picture evocative of the scenes in the newly fashionable "ornamental farm" where sheep and cows grazed in the meadow. Opposite: The Capel Family by C. Johnson c 1639. The influence of French and Dutch garden fashions are seen in the spacious parterre, the statues and the fruit trees trained on the walls. The only flowers are grown in ornamental vases.*

reached its zenith in the gardens of Louis XIV at Versailles. It was a fashion which continued well into the eighteenth century. As late as the 1780's, William Beckford, travelling in Holland, saw gardens with "stiff parterres scrawled and flourished like the embroidery of an old maid's work bag." He may have been thinking of the effect embroiderers created with a linen thread which they knotted using a small shuttle. The thread was then couched down in patterns as elaborate and formal as a real embroidered parterre. The thickness of the thread and the closeness of the knots could be varied and the shuttles were as pretty as fans or pieces of jewellery. They looked charming in use and the

activity was soothing and undemanding, and could be done when the light was too dim for close work. A letter to the *Spectator* humorously suggested that knotting was equally suitable for gentlemen "since it is not inconsistent with any game or other diversion, for it may be done in the play-house, in their coaches, at the tea table . . . and it shows a white hand and diamond ring to great advantage."

The vogue for knotting probably came from Holland and was popular with the ladies at the court of William and Mary. The Queen herself was so fond of the pastime that she is even said to have taken her shuttle with her when she rode in her coach. When the work was couched down on the rich grounds of bedhangings, coverlets, chairs and stools the effect must have been strikingly similar to the formal patterns Queen Mary could see from her windows at Hampton Court where the gardens begun by Charles II had been triumphantly completed under the direction of George London. Both William and Mary were deeply interested in gardening, and at Kensington Palace and Hampton Court they duplicated the splendours of William's palace at Het Loo in Holland. Queen Mary's closet was originally hung with needlework, made by her and the ladies of the court, and as it was situated at the corner of Wren's new building it overlooked both the great semi-circular parterre and the formal gardens in front of the orangery which housed the orange trees brought from the palace of Het Loo. As well as knotting, Queen Mary worked in "satten stitch in worsteds." She and her ladies embroidered exuberant designs in crewel work, whose free flowing patterns like those of knotting, echoed the sweeping curves of box scrollwork in the parterres nearest the palace.

The patterns of crewel work were freer than the exactly matched designs in the parterres but their general appearance was equally bold and vigorous. For the embroiderer they were a welcome change from the exquisite minuteness of blackwork and the precision of canvaswork or stumpwork, yet she could still show off her inventiveness in the decorative treatment of leaves, flowers, fruit, and birds. Early seventeenth century crewel work on both dress and furnishings repeated the patterns and the coiling stems of blackwork but by the middle of the century, the luxuriant

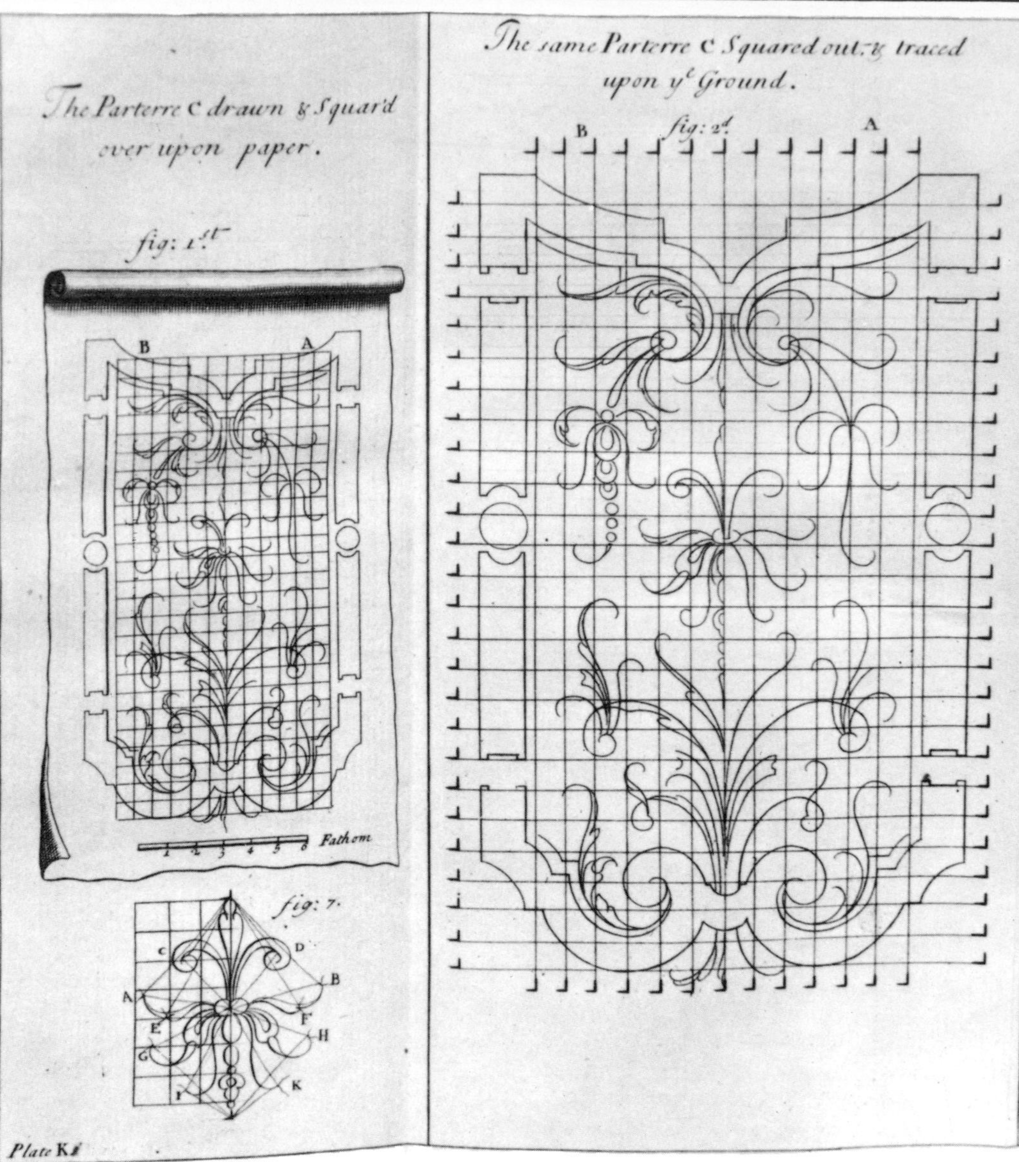

foliage was arranged in far more dynamic designs on hangings which filled the high-ceilinged rooms with swirling leaves and stems, creating yet another form of the perennial "garden within doors." Once again the hangings would outlast the living decorations suggested by Sir Hugh Plat in *The Garden of Eden* in 1675. He proposed that vines should be let in through a window pane and trained all over the room for summer enjoyment.

The effect of a "garden within doors," even fresher and more fanciful than the monochrome crewel work hangings, might also have been created in the late seventeenth century using the bright painted chintzes imported by the East India Company. In 1669 the directors noted the "great practize for printing large branches for hangings" in England, and they began

Above: Diagram from The Theory and Practice of Gardening *by John James illustrating how to enlarge and transfer a parterre pattern to the ground. The book was translated from the French to explain the Grand Manner to English gardeners. The embroiderer uses exactly the same method. The pattern in the margin comes from a contemporary waistcoat whose embroidery resembles the "flourishings" described by London and Wise. Opposite: Canvaswork picture of a garden in the Grand Manner with an elaborate embroidery parterre and Chinoiserie decoration. The patterns in the parterre "cut out curiously into embroidery of flowers and shapes of arabesques" closely resembles one of the designs in* The Garden of Pleasure *by André Mollet seen in the right-hand margin. The embroidered parterres were planted with dwarf box hedges to outline the patterns and the spaces were filled with different coloured earths.*

Courtsey, Museum of Fine Arts, Boston

to send out designs similar to the crewel work branches of stylised oak leaves for the Indian cotton painters to copy and return to England.

When he visited India in the 1660's, the French traveller Bernier was entertained at Delhi by the Great Mughal in his tent which was "lined with Masulipatan chintzes figured expressly for that very purpose with flowers so natural and colours so vivid that the tent seemed to be encompassed with real parterres." Bernier remarked on the variety in the treatment of the painted flowers, many of which must have seemed intriguingly strange to European eyes. The Indian cotton painters were quite unfamiliar with oak leaves and other Western plants and flowers which they found as outlandish as Parkinson's Scythian lamb. Strange distortions took place in the copying. The flowers they produced were transformed into entrancingly novel hybrids even stranger than the real plants newly introduced to Europe, and they were seized on by the embroiderer as striking novelties for exotic garden scenes.

The flowery designs Bernier saw in the Great Mughal's tent may have reminded him not of embroidery parterres, but of "parterres of cutwork" in which flowers were permissible, though even here they were carefully chosen to create uniform effects of colour and height. London and Wise listed eleven different kinds of parterre in their book. Apart from the embroidery parterres, which were nearest to the house and best seen from a specific viewpoint, there were also the flowery cutwork parterres, parterres *à l'anglaise* which

were plain grass plots often used as bowling greens, and water parterres with pools and fountains. These could all be variously combined and London and Wise illustrated their list with plans for gardeners.
In London and Wise's terms the parterres in front of Elizabeth Haines' embroidered house shown on page 73, were "compos'd of Imbroidery and Grass plots which looked very well in little gardens as well as in great." They were further improved by the "fine Dutch jars" planted with shrubs. The "flourishings" and "branch-work," look as if they have been filled in with sand and black earth "different colours serving to set off the Parterre the better."
Old favourites have a tendency to linger on in embroidery just as they do in gardens. In a canvaswork picture showing Esther before Ahasuerus, probably worked at much the same time as Elizabeth Haines' garden, there are the same lumpy trees and ungainly birds typical of seventeenth century needlework. But the embroiderer, in adapting her design from the biblical scene, has had the amusing idea of substituting a house and garden—perhaps her own—for the tragic vignette of the hanging of Esther's kinsman Mordecai which could be glimpsed through the arch in the original engraving.

THE STOKE EDITH HANGINGS

In 1680 Sir William Temple, the celebrated diplomat, retired from public life to devote his time to reading, writing and gardening. In 1685 he bought Moor Park near Farnham in Surrey and settled down to enjoy cultivating the garden and establishing a collection of fruit trees. He and his wife Dorothy Osborn were both nearly 60 but were quite undaunted by the tasks ahead. They were both keen and active gardeners and by 1690, the gardens were in perfect order. In 1692 Sir William published *On the gardens of Epicurus: or of Gardening in the year 1685*, and in this essay he described the Hertfordshire estate belonging to his friend, the Countess of Bedford. This description and the drawing of his own garden in 1690 have much in common with the pair of embroidered hangings shown on pages 74 and 75, formerly at Stoke Edith in Herefordshire but now at Montacute in Somerset. The design of these hangings suggests professional draughtsmanship and the two

Above: Knotting in red silk cord on yellow satin on a chair at Ham House in Surrey. Left: Bird's-eye view of the gardens at Hampton Court. Queen Mary's closet at the corner of the first floor of the palace overlooked the great semi-circular parterre and the formal garden to the left, both completed by London and Wise. Opposite above: Detail from a crewel work hanging with foliage curving as boldly as the "branchwork and flourishings" in the parterres. Below: Elizabeth Haines' picture c 1720 shows a garden with a simple embroidery parterre.

gardens are seen in convincing perspective. If the overall plan of the embroidered garden in the orangery hanging were similar to Moor Park, the area beyond the alley of clipped trees would be the bowling green, clearly marked out as a plain rectangle in the drawing. Bowling greens were considered essential features in any fair-sized garden, the game providing gentle exercise and the plain expanse of the grass making a pleasant contrast to the parterres of embroidery or cutwork.

"In every garden four things are necessary to be provided for, flowers, fruit, shade and water; and whoever lays out a garden without all these, must not pretend it in any perfection: it ought to lie to the best parts of the house . . . so as to be but like one of the rooms out of which you step into another," wrote Sir William. Both the hangings provide these necessities and preserve the intimate atmosphere of "rooms out of which you step into another."

The people enjoying the gardens are wearing the fashions of the 1730's and were probably added at a later date.

Garden houses like the semi-circular one in the teaparty hanging had replaced the

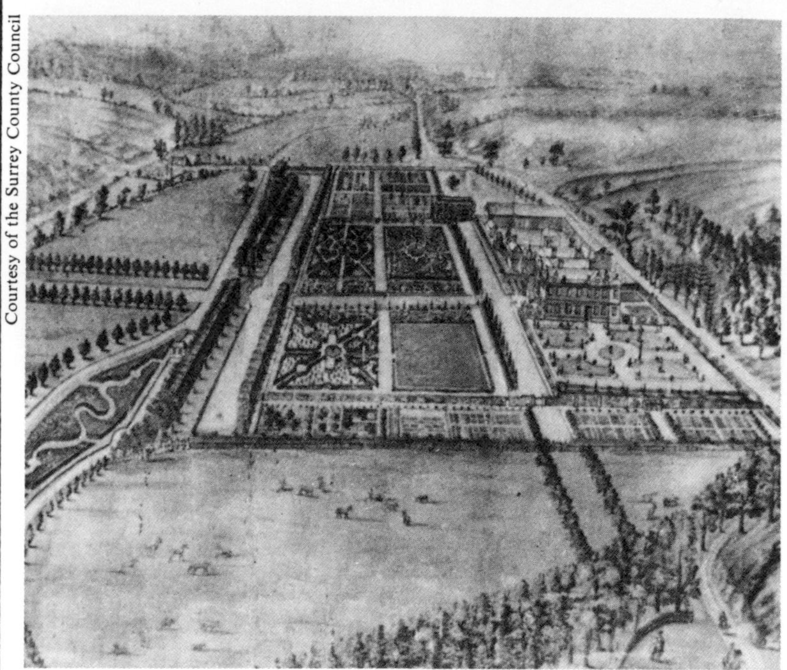

Courtesy of the Surrey County Council

Above: The Orangery Garden, the larger of the Stoke Edith hangings. Left: Engraving of Moor Park in 1690. Opposite above: A teaparty in the smaller Stoke Edith hanging. Opposite below: The frontispiece of the Lady's Recreation *includes many of the features in the Stoke Edith hangings.*

leafy arbours of former days because, as John Worlidge wrote, they were damp, draughty and "on a hot day it is pleasanter to sit under a lime tree than be hood-winked in an arbour." Worlidge suggested siting your garden house "at some remote angle of your garden: For the more remote it is from your house, the more private you will be from the frequent disturbances of your Family and acquaintances."

Borders of pinks and tulips outline the plots in both the hangings. Flowers never really lost their appeal to English gardeners, who compromised with the absolute formality of the French style and adapted it to suit their own taste. In *Campania Foelix: or Rural Delights* published in 1700, Timothy Nourse remarked that seeing a garden without flowers was like sitting down to a meal with the table "furnisht with cloth, Plates and Napkins, and nothing serv'd in . . ." As well as flowers he suggested little bushes of evergreens all through the borders "which would look prettily in winter," and so would little fir trees like the ones set on the outer borders of the orangery hanging.

When he described the Countess of Bedford's garden, Temple particularly admired the wide terrace, the change of levels, the borders set with standard laurels and the orange trees. The main parterre was reached by descending some stone steps. It was divided into quarters with gravel walks and adorned with "Two Fountains and Eight Statues," and prob-

ably looked very similar to the garden in the teaparty hanging. Lead statues, like clipped greens, were another Dutch fashion made popular by William and Mary.
Oranges had been grown in England since the sixteenth century but they were still a rare treat in 1666 when Pepys "pulled off a little one by stealth" and ate it in Lord Brooke's garden at Hackney. Sir William would have seen magnificent orangeries at The Hague and in France, but he declared that his trees were as large as almost any he had seen and as laden with flowers and fruit. In his own garden he set the trees on pedestals against a south wall, but as in the small hanging, most gardeners put them in pots along the paths. Temple was famous for his skill in training fruit trees—the Moor Park apricot tree can still be bought today. The two trees nearest the summer house in the teaparty hanging, beautifully espaliered on the warm brick wall and covered with ripe if premature fruit, show how lovely they could be as a garden feature, softening the formality yet in keeping with it.
The Stoke Edith hangings are a fascinating record of the English formal garden in its heyday. The wrought iron gates at the entrance to the orangery garden are typical of the period. Magnificent surviving examples can still be seen in the Fountain Garden at Hampton Court made by the French smith Jean Tijou, their scrolling patterns echoing the box embroidery that once adorned the parterres. The gate piers too are characteristic garden features. In the Stoke Edith hanging they are surmounted by heraldic lions reminiscent of the stumpwork "beastes" but more elegant and formal. Simpler versions can be seen in Elizabeth Haines' embroidery on page 73, and at the end of the garden in the Esther and Asahuerus picture on page 65.

GEORGIAN GARDENS

All that luxurious fancy can invent
What poets feign and painters represent

Anonymous poem
addressed to Lord Carlisle, 1733

THE LURE OF CHINOISERIE

In 1694 Sarah Thurstone completed a coverlet in brilliant coloured silks on white satin. Right in the middle she placed a tiny figure who, apart from some familiar details like oak trees, roses, and a friendly snail or two, is alone in a world as alluringly strange as those to be seen decorating the lustrous surfaces of lacquer cabinets and porcelain vases. Around him the gay pavilions with pennants fluttering from their fanciful roofs, and balconies of delicate fretwork conjure up the world of far Cathay which had entranced the Western imagination since the days of Marco Polo. This remote land resembled a paradise garden more sophisticated and elegant than the Garden of Eden and even richer in mysterious decorative motifs. Whether their origin was Chinese, Japanese or Indian, they were found equally intriguing.

Porcelain vases and lacquer cabinets were much in vogue when Sarah Thurstone made her quilt, and they can be seen fashionably piled one on top of the other in the canvaswork panel on page 79. The accompanying panel next to it brings together many more favourite Chinoiserie motifs—pavilions, bridges, blossoming trees and birds. The embroiderer used the decorative elements of Chinoiserie to create frivolous garden vignettes which were vaguely but deliciously oriental in mood. In the seventeenth century these creations had no counterpart in real gardens, except perhaps in pheasantries where rare birds were kept, less striking in appearance than the dazzling creatures of needlework. Similar birds preen themselves on the Indian chintzes and Chinese embroideries whose "splendour and vividness," according to John Evelyn, "excell anything yet seen in Europe." The embroiderer drew inspiration from them and from the tapestries, wallpapers and lacquerwork to be seen in fashionable houses. The refulgent surface of lacquer made the garden vignettes seem even more mysterious and appealing, and soon an imitation lacquer was developed so that amateurs could do their own "japanning." This soon became a craze for which books of vaguely oriental designs were quickly produced to make the pastime easier for those with little talent for drawing.

Stalker and Parker produced their *Treatise on Japanning and Varnishing* in 1688, and the motifs were equally useful for em-

Hanging with English flowers in Chinoiserie vase embroidered in wools on worsted, second quarter of the eighteenth century. Flowers in ornamental containers, especially exotics brought out from the greenhouse in summer, and evergreens were a feature of gardens in the Grand Manner. They can also be seen in the Stoke Edith hangings and in the Formal Garden on page 71.

SARAH·THVRSTONE
16
94

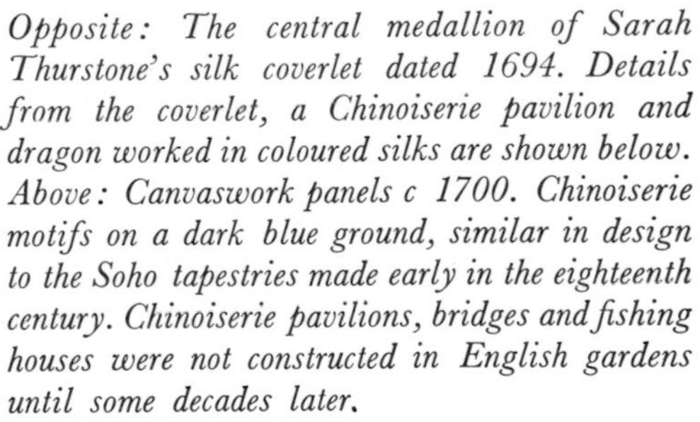

Opposite: The central medallion of Sarah Thurstone's silk coverlet dated 1694. Details from the coverlet, a Chinoiserie pavilion and dragon worked in coloured silks are shown below. Above: Canvaswork panels c 1700. Chinoiserie motifs on a dark blue ground, similar in design to the Soho tapestries made early in the eighteenth century. Chinoiserie pavilions, bridges and fishing houses were not constructed in English gardens until some decades later.

broiderers in search of pavilions and pagodas. More authentic views of Chinese buildings and garden features might also have been seen and adapted from the illustrations in *The Embassy to the Grand Tartar* by the Dutchman John Nieuhof, which caused immense excitement when it was translated into English in 1669. There were pagodas galore, and strange artificial hills similar to the twisted rocks on Sarah Thurstone's quilt, and the peculiar outcrops at the bottom of the canvas panel shown on page 79. Nieuhof found the rocks one of the most exciting features of Chinese gardens.

"There is not anything wherein the Chinese show their ingenuity more than these rocks and Artificial Hills which are so curiously wrought that Art seems to exceed Nature. These Cliffs are made of a sort of stone, and sometimes of Marble, and so rarely adorned with Trees and Flowers that all that see them are surprised with admiration."

These rocks also appeared in crewel embroidery, and most charmingly of all, in whitework, where they were ingeniously patterned and cut out into small caverns sheltering diminutive animals and plants. The whitework scenes convey the airy flimsiness of Chinoiserie which characterised the real fishermen's houses, bridges and pavilions that were beginning to appear in the eighteenth century gardens. It was the irregularity of Chinese gardens that first intrigued English garden designers. Sir William Temple was the first to discuss it, contrasting what he had heard of Chinese designs with the regularity of Western gardens. "Among us, the beauty of building and planting is placed chiefly in some certain proportions, symmetries, or uniformities, our walks and trees ranged so, as to answer one another, and at exact distances. The

Chinese scorn this way of planting . . . their imagination is employed in contriving Figures, where the Beauty shall be great, and strike the eye, but without any order or Disposition of Parts, that shall be commonly or easily observed. And though we have hardly any Notion of this sort of Beauty, yet they have a particular Word to express it . . . they say the *Sharawadgi* is fine or is admirable . . . And whoever observes the work upon the best *Indian* gowns, or the painting upon their best Skreens or Purcellans, will find their beauty is all of this kind."

Sir William did not advise English gardeners to follow suit "they are adventures of too hard achievement of any common hands"—and the odds were twenty to one that they would fail, "whereas in regular figures, 'tis hard to make any great and remarkable faults." Contrary to this advice, in his own garden Sir William laid out the area beyond the formal parterres and bowling green in an asymmetrical design with a serpentine path winding through trees.

Designs resembling the painted chintzes of the best Indian gowns decorate the extraordinary dress shown on page 81, possibly adapted from bedhangings embroidered in the early decades of the eighteenth century but not made up until the 1750's. By then Chinoiserie buildings, some as strange and ramshackle as those in embroidery, had begun to appear in English gardens. "There are several paltry Chinese buildings and bridges which have the merit or demerit of being the progenitors of a very numerous race all over the Kingdom," wrote Horace Walpole in 1753. Three years previously he was less disparaging, saying that these "dispersed buildings" gave a "whimsical air of novelty that is very pleasing." Anyone seeing the pagoda at Kew Gardens in London is likely to be struck by its "whimsical air" even though it has lost the tinkling bells and golden dragons that once decorated the painted roofs. Visitors to Kew in the 1760's would also have been able to see the enchanting Chinoiserie pavilion set in a lake with a fretwork bridge. This was constructed in the Pheasant Garden by Sir William Chambers, the pagoda's designer, who was considered an authority on such buildings as he had actually been to China.

As in embroidery, so in gardens: designers used the decorative features of Chinoiserie arranging them in a frivolous manner remote from the complexity and symbolism of real Chinese gardens like those

Below: "Cliffs made by Art" from The Embassy to the Grand Tartar *by John Nieuhof translated in 1669. These artificial hills "adorned with trees and flowers" were much admired in Chinese gardens. The book contained many illustrations of pagodas and other exotic buildings seen in Chinese towns.*

surrounding the Imperial Palace at Peking. At Stourhead in Wiltshire a wealthy amateur designer, Henry Hoare, created a marvellous lake from the old seventeenth century fish ponds. Along the two walks that encircled it he cunningly placed a series of garden buildings ranging in mood from the grandeur of the Pantheon to the simplicity of the rustic cottage and the oriental whimsicality of the Turkish tent, the Chinese Parasol and the dainty Chinese bridge. The last three soon collapsed, but the grotto, as wonderfully fanciful as Nieuhof's artificial hills or the embroiderer's strangest adaptations of them, remains as mysterious as when it was made.

RURAL LANDSKIPS

In October 1714 a letter appeared in the *Spectator* from a "venerable correspondent" at the end of her patience with two gadabout nieces. "Their dress, their tea, their visits take up all their time, and they go to bed as tired with doing nothing as I am after quilting a whole underpetticoat . . . Those hours which in this age are thrown away in dress, play, visits and the like, were employed in my time in writing out receipts, or working beds, chairs and hangings for the family. For my part I have plied the needle these fifty years, and by my good will would never have it out of my hand. It grieves my heart to see a couple of proud idle flirts sipping their tea, for a whole afternoon, in a room hung around with the industry of their great grandmothers. Pray, sir, take the laudable mystery of embroidery into your serious consideration."

Joseph Addison, the editor of the *Spectator* could not resist poking fun at the industrious aunt and her two idle charges and he answered, tongue in cheek: "What a delightful entertainment must it be to the fair sex, whom their native modesty, and the tenderness of men towards them, exempts from public business, to pass their hours in imitating fruits and flowers, and transplanting all the beauties of nature into their own dress, or raising a new creation in their closets and apartments? How pleasing is the amusement of walking among the shades and groves planted by themselves, in surveying heroes slain by their needle, or little cupids which they have brought into the world without pain?

"This is, methinks, the most proper way wherein a lady can shew a fine genius, and I cannot forbear wishing, that several writers of that sex had chosen to apply themselves rather to tapestry than rhyme.

Below left: Detail from an eighteenth century whitework apron with a fisherman seated on a rock. Below right: Chinoiserie buildings set among "artificial hills rarely adorned with trees and flowers." Details of embroidery in silks and metal threads on an open robe. An avenue of trees appears on the same dress.

Your pastoral poetesses may vent their fancy in rural landscapes, and place despairing shepherds under silken willows, or drown them in a stream of mohair."

It is curious that no "pastoral poetesses" with a taste for embroidery wrote in to remind Addison that just over two years previously in June 1712, he had already used his magazine to express his views on rural landscape in far more persuasive terms: "Why may not a whole Estate be thrown into a kind of Garden by frequent Plantations, that may turn as much to the Profit, as the Pleasure of the Owner? A Marsh overgrown with Willows, or a Mountain shaded with Oaks, are not only more beautiful, but more beneficial, than when they lie bare and unadorned. Fields of Corn make a pleasant Prospect, and if the Walks were a little taken care of that lie between them, if the natural Embroidery of the Meadows were helpt and improved by some small Additions of Art, and the several Rows of Hedges set off by Trees and Flowers, that the Soil was capable of receiving, a Man might make a pretty Landskip of his own Possessions."

Addison was expressing the growing disenchantment with gardens, like those in the Stoke Edith hangings "laid out by Rule and Line." "Our British Gardeners instead of humouring Nature, love to deviate from it as much as possible. Our Trees rise in Cones, Globes, and Pyramids. We see the Marks of the Scissars upon

Wooburn Farm in Surrey. "With the beauties which enliven a garden are everywhere intermixed many properties of a farm." Whately's description is equally apt for the pastoral scenes in eighteenth century needlework. Opposite: Canvaswork picture of a family group and their house in a rustic garden setting.

every Plant and Bush. I do not know whether I am singular in my Opinion, but for my own part, I would rather look upon a Tree in all its Luxuriancy and Diffusion of Boughs and Branches, than when it is thus cut and trimmed into a Mathematical Figure; and cannot but fancy that an Orchard in Flower looks infinitely more delightful, than all the little Labyrinths of the most finished Parterre."

Addison's plea for a freer and more natural style of gardening, was taken up by Pope whose essay on *Verdant Sculpture* had appeared in 1713, and in 1731 he wittily expressed his distaste for the rigidity of the formal garden in the *Epistle to Lord Burlington*.

"Tired of the scene Parterres
and Fountains yield,
He finds at last he better likes a field."

During the early years of the century the countryside changed dramatically as a result of Government policy to enclose the common land and improve turf for grazing. Gradually a patchwork of well-kept fields divided by hedges spread over land that had formerly been bog or "all horrid

The Metropolitan Museum of Art, Gift of Irwin Untermeyer, 1964

and woody," and thickets were planted for the benefit of huntsmen who now chased after devious foxes instead of galloping headlong down straight drives after stags. The countryside was no longer hostile; it was as well ordered as the land within the garden walks, but it avoided the "mathematical Exactness and crimping stiffness" of rigidly imposed designs. The novel idea of merging garden and countryside, making a "pretty Landskip of your own possessions," appealed not only to the imagination, but to the pocket. Garden owners, tired of the "Lothsome Burden" of expense in maintaining their parterres of embroidery, their miles of clipped hedges and their exotic "greens," were probably swayed as much by thoughts of economy as by boredom with the old style when they decided to dig up the parterres and cut down the avenues.

The argument of economy was temptingly proposed by Stephen Switzer in 1715 in the *Nobleman, Gentleman and Gardener's Recreation.* He recommended that "all the adjacent country should be laid open to the view of the eye and should not be bounded by high walls," and named the device that made this practical and possible,the haha, which he described as "an easy unaffected manner of Fencing to make the adjacent country look as if it were all a garden." He left out the essential information that the fence was to be sunk below eye level in a ditch which kept cattle and sheep away from the vicinity of the house, but gave the inhabitants the illusion that the land beyond it was part of the garden.

There is no knowing whether there are hahas in the "pretty rural landskips" of contemporary pictorial needlework, for they would be easily concealed behind the rows of hillocks that at first sight appear to resemble those of the previous century. Nor has the embroiderer abandoned the cast of biblical and mythological personages, but new ones have been added—skittishly dressed as nymphs and shepherds whose flocks of sheep and goats have replaced the strange spotted beasts roaming the seventeenth century gardens. Embroiderers embraced Addison's serious and frivolous suggestions, "raising a new creation in their closets and apartments" where rural landscapes appeared in pictures, as panels for sconces and screens, inside card tables and ingeniously covering the entire surface of elegant upholstered wing chairs. Canvaswork was back in fashion and once again the embroidered scenes worked on furnishings throughout the house echoed a child's eye view of the latest gardens which were now being laid out to give the illusion of an arcadian landscape as idealised as the paintings of Claude.

"Landscape should contain variety enough to form a picture upon canvas; and this is no bad test, as I think the landscape

painter is the gardener's best designer," wrote William Shenstone in his *Unconnected Thoughts on Gardening* published in 1764. He put his theory into practice at his own retreat, the Leasowes near Halesowen. Wealthier garden owners tried even harder than Shenstone to recreate the Claudian landscapes which hung in their country houses as evocative mementoes of the Italian scenery with its classical ruins which they had admired on the Grand Tour. Shenstone had never been to Italy and he contented himself by evoking the spirit of the idyllic painted landscapes, ingeniously re-organising his estate, so that the visitor had the pleasure of walking from one viewpoint to another, enjoying a series of carefully contrived scenes. "A rural scene to me is never perfect without the addition of some kind of building," he wrote, and these were sited along the path. There were cottages which were pleasing on account of their variety and "the tranquillity that seems to reign there."

The colourful scenes of rural life in eighteenth century canvaswork, with their cheerful cottages, quite unlike the preposterous toy castles of the previous century, set in the folds of rolling hills alternately golden and green like cornfields and meadows, topped by windmills and clumps of trees evoke the idyllic tranquillity of

Left: Print, "A view of the Palace from the Lawn in the Royal Garden at Kew." Below: Embroidered picture based on the print and embroidered in tent and cross stitch on canvas. Sir William Chambers laid out Kew Gardens for Princess Augusta of Wales in the late 1750's combining the picturesque elements of an ornamental farm with classical and exotic garden buildings. Opposite: Canvaswork pictures c 1720 with figures dressed as frivolously as the nymphs and shepherds of Boucher or Watteau.

The Metropolitan Museum of Art, Gift of Irwin Untermeyer, 1964

gardens like the Leasowes.

In 1735 Philip Southcote bought Wooburn Farm in Surrey and laid out the grounds as an ornamental farm. His original desire for making improvements was "joined to a taste for the more simple delights of the country . . . as a means of bringing every rural circumstance within the verge of the garden." The success of his venture was vividly described by Thomas Whateley in 1770 in *Observations on Modern Gardening:* "With the beauties which enliven a garden are everywhere intermixed many properties of a farm; both the lawns are fed (grazed), and the lowing of the herds, the bleating of the sheep, and the tinkling of the bell-wether resound all round the plantations; even the clucking of poultry is not omitted; for a menagerie of very simple design is placed near the Gothic building; a small serpentine river is provided for the waterfowl, while the others stray among the flowering shrubs on the bank or straggle about on the neighbouring lawn; and the cornfields are the subject of every rural employment, which arable land from seed time to harvest can furnish."

A path led round the farm, and "the scenes through which it leads are truly elegant, everywhere rich, and always agreeable. A peculiar cheerfulness overspreads the lawns arising from the number and splendour of objects with which they abound, the inequalities of the ground and the varieties of the plantation."

The charm of the gardens at Wooburn Farm and every detail of their appearance is matched in the embroidered scenes. They evoke carefree summer days when time steals away, and it is pleasant to rest on the grass listening to the sound of the shepherd's pipe, and water flowing along a "little wandering rill" arranged to run in the same manner as it would do in a field "so that it generally passes through banks of violets and primroses . . . that seem to be of its own choosing" like the stream in Addison's garden. English flowers had returned to the green slopes of the needlework hills, and often encircled the scenes with lavish blooms, like those which grew in the borders of herbaceous plants packed with hollyhocks, honesty, stocks, sweet Williams, Canterbury bells, scabious and pinks at Wooburn Farm.

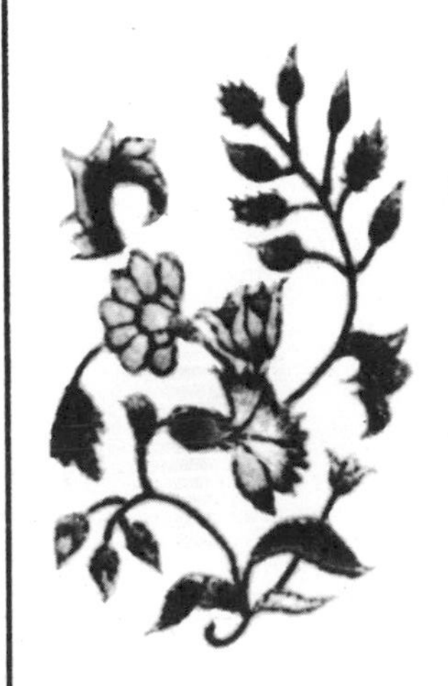

These flower beds were "rather too profusely strewed" in Whateley's view, and they were quite unlike anything to be found in other landscape gardens where grass "wrapt all in everlasting green."

The gardens surrounding the White House at Kew shown on page 84, were similar to Wooburn Farm, in that a walk enclosing meadows with grazing cattle and sheep led from one viewpoint to another. In the garden laid out by Sir William Chambers for Princess Augusta of Wales, mother of George III, there were classical buildings, a greenhouse for the Princess, exotic plants—some of which have been stood outside, their formality contrasting with the trees growing naturally opposite them—and the pagoda and menagarie.

The number of single palm trees among the oaks, and the oriental birds amid the poultry in eighteenth century needlework suggest that the embroiderer also found it amusing to introduce a note of strangeness in the most English rural scenes. Embroidered shepherds and shepherdesses were dressed up in clothes as extravagant and frivolous as those painted by Boucher and Watteau, which like all the other trimmings of the ornamental farm "betray more wealthy expense than is consistent with the economy of a Farmer, or the rusticity of labour." This was Horace Walpole's opinion and he went on, "Mr Southcote's ornamental farm where he displayed his peculiar style with happiness and taste is the habitation of such nymphs and shepherds as are represented in landscapes and novels, but do not exist in real life." Yet silken shepherds and shepherdesses might have been seen in real eighteenth century gardens taking part in the fêtes champêtres as enthusiastically as their ancestors had done in the masques and revels of previous centuries.

Mrs Delany, diarist, embroiderer, maker of gardens, shell grottoes, paper mosaics, and inveterate party-goer described a ball at Delville near Dublin in 1752 "with musicians and singers dressed like arcadian shepherds and shepherdesses placed among the rocks." In July 1774 she enjoyed the "fairy scene" at Lady Betty Hamilton's fête champêtre: "The company was received in the lawn before the house, which is scattered with trees and opens to the downs. The company arriving, and partys of people of all ranks that came to admire, made the scene quite enchanting, which was greatly enlivened with a most beautiful setting sun breaking from a black cloud in its greatest glory. After half an hour's sauntering the company were called to the other side, to a more confined spot, where benches were placed in a semicircle, and a fortunate clump of trees in the centre of the small lawn hid a band of musick; a stage was (supposed to be formed) by a part being divided from the other part of the garden, with sticks entwined with natural flowers in wreaths and festoons joining each. A little dialogue between a Shepherd and Shepherdess, with a welcome to the company, was sung and said, and dancing by 16 men and 16 women figuranti's from the Opera lasted about half an hour; after which this party was employed in swinging, jumping, shooting with bows and arrows, and various country sports. The gentlemen and ladies danced on the green till it was dark, and then preceded the musick to the other side of the garden . . . People in general very elegantly dressed: the very young as peasants; the next as Polonise; the matrons dominos; the men principally dominos and *many gardeners*, as in the Opera dances."

DEAR MRS DELANY

"But here the needle plies its busy task,
The pattern grows,
the well-depict'd flower
Unfolds its bosom, buds and leaves
and sprigs,
And curling tendrils,
gracefully disposed,
Follow the nimble fingers of the fair;
A wreath that cannot fade,
of flowers that blow
With most success
when all besides decay."

William Cowper finished this poem *The Task* in 1784 when Mrs Delany was eighty-four years old. Throughout her long life her needle "plied its busy task" in embroidery that was extraordinarily varied and individual. She worked in white on the finest lawn and muslin, and with coloured silks and worsteds specially made for her in Ireland, on canvas, silk and woollen grounds. She also enjoyed knotting and spinning, and she helped her second husband, Doctor Delany, in making their garden at Delville at Glasnevin near Dublin. Though her needlework is dispersed, and Delville is destroyed, some of her sketches remain, with her journal and her abundant letters.

Above: Central medallion of a quilt worked by Mrs Delany in knotting couched on Irish linen. It was given to Thomas Sandford on his birthday in 1765. Far right: Silhouette in paper of Mrs Delany c 1770. Mrs Delany was famous for her own cut-paper flowers.

Like Gerard and Parkinson, Mrs Delany valued the links between embroidery and gardens. She described a dress worn by the Duchess of Queensberry which sounds as overwhelming as the petticoat shown on page 81, and it must surely have been the embroidery that impressed her rather than the overall effect.

"The Duchess of Queensberry's clothes pleased me best. They were white satin embroidered, the bottom of the petticoat *brown hills* covered with all sorts of weeds, and every breadth had an *old stump of a tree* that ran up almost to the top of the petticoat, broken and ragged, and worked with brown chenille, round which were twined nasturtiums, ivy, honeysuckles, periwinkles, convolvuluses, and all sorts of twining flowers, which spread and covered the petticoat."

Mrs Delany's underlining of an "old stump of a tree" suggests that she might, like Walpole, be poking fun at the landscape gardener William Kent who was so determined to imitate nature "that he had planted dead trees in Kensington Gardens to give a greater truth to the scene." Kent's ruling principle was that "Nature abhors a straight line", and in gardens, as in embroidery, this principle led to much pretty meandering. "A serpentine river and a wood are become the absolute necessities of life," wrote Walpole. Like the sinuous rivers, streams and paths in the landscape garden, the stems, foliage and flowers on dresses, carpets and hangings twisted and turned as naturally as if they had been tossed from a shepherdess's basket onto the ground. Lady Llanover described a petticoat of Mrs Delany's, "covered with sprays of natural flowers, in different positions, including the bugloss, auriculas, honeysuckle, wild roses, lilies of the valley, yellow and white jessamine, interspersed with small single flowers. The border at the bottom being entirely composed of large flowers, in the manner in which they grow, both *garden* and *wild* flowers being intermingled where the

form, proportions and foliage rendered it desirable for the effect of the whole."

Lady Llanover constantly drew attention to the naturalness of Mrs Delany's work, but her own and Mrs Delany's descriptions of it suggest that her real gift lay in absorbing what she saw and then formalising it to suit a particular piece of work choosing perfectly appropriate stitches and materials. Her originality and skill can still be admired in the flowers she cut from coloured paper and mounted on a black ground, an activity she did not begin till her seventies.

Mrs Delany's aptitude for design was linked with her skill at drawing, and her sketches record the picturesque appeal of her garden at Delville. The garden was eleven acres in size, too small by eighteenth century standards to be an ornamental farm, though there were deer, meandering streams and an island with swans. The Delanys often took their meals out of doors where an Irish harpist played to them and where the profusion of flowers bloomed as naturally as on her own petticoat. They grew quantities of different fruits, and in 1750 Mrs Delany was "considering about a green house." She

Collection of Mrs Ruth Hadyn

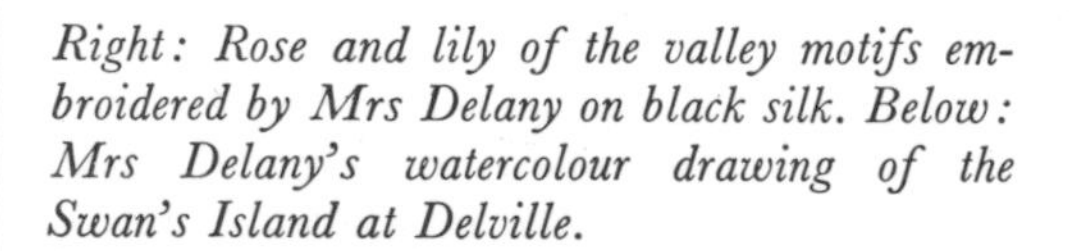

Right: Rose and lily of the valley motifs embroidered by Mrs Delany on black silk. Below: Mrs Delany's watercolour drawing of the Swan's Island at Delville.

wrote "I believe I shall build one this spring; my orange trees thrive *so well* they deserve one." They made a "nine pin bowling alley for very merry exercise" and entertained their numerous friends. Sadly their taste for trying out novelties and making improvements ended in financial disaster and when he died in 1768 Doctor Delany was:

"Quite ruin'd and bankrupt
reduced to a farthing:
By making too much of
a very small garden."

Mrs Delany returned to England after his death and contented herself with other peoples' gardens, especially those of her closest friend the Duchess of Portland, at Bulstrode near Gerrards Cross. The Duchess shared many of her interests and together they botanized, sketched and enjoyed each other's conversation, while Mrs Delany sat at her spinning wheel or embroidery, or made candelabras of shellwork for her friend's house. Her enthusiastic delight in something new is typical, as is the perfection of her technique, and her perseverance in carrying it out. Yet even she sometimes found the completion of a piece of work tedious. "It is provoking," she wrote, "to have the ground take up so much more time than the flowers," a thought that often crosses any gardener's mind at the start of a weeding session.

PLEASING MELANCHOLY

In the spring of 1733, Mrs Delany, then Mrs Pendarves, was in Ireland staying with Mr Wesley whose garden boasted three canals, each with a different pleasure boat and "a fir-grove, dedicated to Vesta, in the midst of which is her statue; at some distance from it is a mound covered with evergreens, on which is placed a temple with the statue of Apollo. Neptune, Proserpine, Diana, all have due honours paid them, and Fame has been too good a friend to the master of all these improvements to be neglected; her Temple is near the house, at the end of a terrace, near which the four Seasons take their stand, very well represented by Flora, Ceres, Bacchus, and an old gentleman with a hood on his head, warming his hands over a fire."

Statues, temples, urns, grottoes, even hermitages complete with suitably unkempt hermits were sited in different parts of the landscape garden to indicate different moods and associations. There were ruins and urns at both the Leasowes and Wooburn Farm designed to turn the visitors' thoughts from frivolity to melancholy. Passing by open cornfields and

Patterns for embroidery including many of the "objects" used by landscape gardeners to inspire "pleasing melancholy" such as temples, urns and monuments.

Collection of M. Davis-Goff

Ruins were an essential part of pleasing melancholy. Right: "Petit Autel presque Ruiné" from Jardins Anglo-Chinois *by Le Rouge. Above left: Garden temple embroidered on white satin in silks and metal threads. Above right: Detail from a late eighteenth century picture on silk of girls by an urn reminiscent of Le Rouge's altar monument beside a lake in a landscape garden. The background is painted and only simple flat stitches are used.*

happy rural scenes, suddenly they would come upon a shaded sylvan temple, or a solitary garlanded urn, complete with an inscription recalling the death of some dearly loved friend.

"A ruin," wrote Shenstone, "may be neither new to us, nor majestic, nor beautiful, yet afford the pleasing melancholy which proceeds from a reflection on decayed magnificence. For this reason an able gardener should avail himself of objects that convey reflections of the pleasing kind." At the Leasowes the hilly ground made it easy to arrange the objects to prompt ever-changing emotions as one walked round the estate.

The embroiderer is always looking for new motifs and new materials for working them. In the second half of the eighteenth century, she adopted the" objects" used by the landscape gardener, arranging them to create miniature prospects of silken temples overhung by chenille willows, and urns and monuments set in glades visited

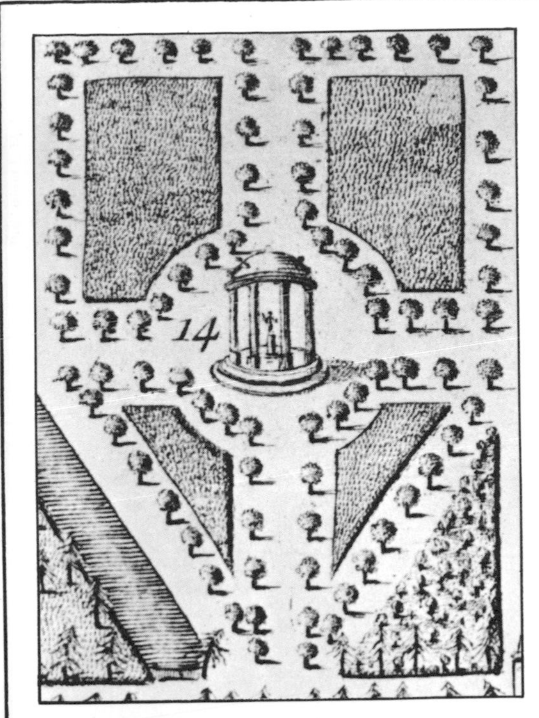

Above: Temple from a garden plan from Jardins Anglo-Chinois *by Le Rouge. Le Rouge's many books of designs published in the 1770's and 1780's form a record of changing garden fashions in the eighteenth century. Garden temples, many of them based on the temple of the Sibyl at Tivoli, were built in all the important landscape gardens. Right: A picture embroidered on silk. Fame strewing flowers on Shakespeare's tomb. The trees are worked in chenille.*

by mournful maidens bringing flowers and garlands. The rural landscapes were not entirely abandoned, but scenes of "pleasing melancholy" were worked on silk backgrounds using simple flat stitches in silks and chenilles whose fragility made them suitable only to be framed as pictures or panels for screens. As in the past, the designs often came from engravings and book illustrations, but now a single incident or view was preferred to the composite pictures and stories of earlier days. Background details such as the sky or distant mountains, and the faces and hands of the figures were painted on the silk in watercolour. Some patterns were available ready-drawn, but if they did not appeal, the embroiderer could probably find what she wanted in the books of designs for garden buildings and ornaments, or in novels or volumes of poetry, for the same motifs were widespread. They appeared in paintings, furniture, silver and plasterwork in fashionable houses. She found "melancholy" in pleasing or thrilling quantities as she lingered over the stanzas of Gray's *Elegy*, wept over Goethe's tragic story of Werther's love for Charlotte, and revelled in the *Mysteries of Udolpho* by Mrs Radcliffe.

It was tempting to illustrate the romantic scenes in needlework, and most fortunate that this could be done quickly and without a great deal of skill when there were other delightful pastimes such as sketching to dabble in. Generally embroiderers preferred small-scale picturesque vignettes of the landscape garden, and sensibly, made few attempts to convey either the vastness of the famous landscape gardens laid out by Capability Brown or the paintings of the great landscape artists—Claude and Gaspard—which garden designers had imitated in three-dimensional form in the English countryside. The only notable exception was Miss Morritt of Rokeby who endeavoured to reproduce in her "needlepaintings" in worsted in long and short stitch, the landscapes of Gaspard Poussin.

In 1760 Mrs Delany visited Longleat where the formal garden had been removed in favour of "a fine lawn, a serpentine river, wooded hills, gravel paths meandering round a shrubbery, all modernised by the ingenious and much sought after Mr Brown." Not everyone was as enthusiastic and, as in the days of topiary and rigid formality, satirists now found that there were just as many absurdities in the landscape garden. Their witty comments sometimes correspond with contemporary pictorial embroidery, with its naive or frivolous air even in supposedly serious scenes.

The garden created by the newly rich Mr Sterling in Garrick and Colman's play *The Clandestine Marriage* of 1766 has echoes in embroidery in the choice and overcrowding of decorative elements. Besides a "little Gothic dairy, an octagonal summer house, a Chinese Bridge, a cascade and ruins which had cost one hundred and fifty pounds to put into repair," there was also a mock spire among distant trees masquerading as a parish church. "One must always have a church, or an obelisk, or something to terminate the prospect, you know . . ."

A tottering obelisk terminates the prospect in a canvaswork chair seat copied from an illustration by John Wootton of one of John Gay's *Fables*, and another illustration in the same series, also adapted as a chair seat, was designed by William Kent. This was the fable of *The Poet and the Rose* in which Kent chose the moment where the gesturing poet is about to pluck the rose, who objects as loudly as Alice's Tiger Lily, reminding him that her flowers are indispensable to poets and that they should not be idly picked and left to die. Both engraving and embroidery wittily convey the teasing irony of the poem, and the contrived and crowded setting, with its statue, fountain and tree, would be equally apt to illustrate the glade in the garden of Squire Mushroom, another would-be amateur of taste, mocked in the periodical

The World in 1753. "After traipsing along the yellow serpentine river" past a hermitage built of roots, his guests "almost in despair of ever visiting daylight any more," emerged "on a sudden into an open and circular area richly chequered with beds of flowers and embellished with a little fountain playing in the centre of it."

The most amusing critic of the landscape garden in all its phases was Thomas Love Peacock. "I perceive," says Mr Milestone, the hero of his satirical novel *Headlong Hall* (published in 1816), that "these grounds have never been touched by the finger of taste," and he asks the owner for permission "to wave the wand of enchantment" over them so that they are instantly transformed by a gamut of decorative devices. There were many gardeners in the eighteenth century whose grounds remained "untouched by the finger of taste" and who went on cultivating flowers as enthusiastically as they had done in the past. The flood of plant introductions continued and some, like the pelargonium introduced in 1701, were taken up by the embroiderer—Mrs Delany introduced them on her black petticoat. But apart from the profusion of imaginary oriental flowers, the embroiderer remained most faithful to old favourites like roses, carnations and tulips. These are at their most charming when they frame a pastoral landscape—a cottage with meadows and a stream, like the scene described by Jane Austen in *Emma*. "It was a sweet view—sweet to the eye and the mind. English verdure, English culture, English comfort, seen under a sun bright, without being oppressive."

Opposite: Canvaswork chair seat adapted from an illustration depicting the Poet and the Rose *from John Gay's* Fables *of 1727. Below: Adaptation of John Wootton's illustration for the Fable of the* Gardener and the Hog. *The gardener "of peculiar taste" who made a friend of his pet hog and allowed it to share his house and table, attacks the animal who has just devoured all the prize tulips. Urns similar to these and to the obelisk can be seen in the gardens of Lord Burlington's villa at Chiswick laid out in the 1720's with the help of William Kent.*

VICTORIAN GARDENS

Unmistakeable suggestions of gardens

William Morris

CARPET BEDDING
AND BERLIN WOOLWORK

In the last years of the eighteenth century many gardens had become so "natural" that critics claimed they were indistinguishable from the surrounding countryside. Capability Brown's most famous follower, Humphry Repton, gradually allowed slight formal elements to reappear near to the house, and many garden owners in the early 1800's seized on this with enthusiasm. Flower beds near the house were reintroduced; Brown's lawns were kept at bay with terraces; formal trelliswork festooned with roses, jasmine and honeysuckle matched the symmetry of the neo-classical architecture; and even the long banished fountain, symbol of artifice and unnatural constraint, was allowed to return.

In the 1820's this development was particularly welcome to the growing, affluent and educated middle classes. Their properties were not large enough to embrace the spacious wildness of the landscape garden, but they could and did enjoy both the picturesque effects, derived from sentimental delight in "pleasing melancholy" and the rediscovered advantages of formality. A wave of literature—magazines and handbooks—fed the gardening appetites of householders, instructing and encouraging the creators of gardens surrounding the new suburban "villas". Such gardens might be small but they would also be neat, regular and even formal, thus demonstrating the owner's diligence and responsibility.

In 1841 a reader wrote to the *Ladies Magazine of Gardening* with this query: "I am desirous of gaining a little information as to the planting of a geometrical flower garden with the *gayest* and *brightest* colours." Mrs Loudon, the editor answered her question: "The situation having been chosen, the ground must be levelled, and the plan, if complicated traced upon it. Having divided the plan into an equal number of squares by lines drawn on the paper, copy what is found on a large scale in every square. This is difficult to describe, but it will be easy in practice to anyone who has been accustomed to copying worsted work patterns drawn on Berlin paper."

At this date, few of Mrs Loudon's readers would have been unfamiliar with copying patterns for Berlin woolwork. As the Countess of Wilton noted in *The Art of Needlework*, the first history of embroidery,

Opposite above: Victorian garden from E. A. Brooke's Gardens of England *of 1856. Below left: Berlin woolwork picture of a fountain framed by a border of plush stitch flowers. Below right: Fountains marked the return of formality. Illustration from one of Mrs Loudon's articles in* The Ladies Companion.

Collection of Mrs Humphrey Brand

IS
KF
Say first, of God above, or man below,
What can we reason, but from what we know?
Of man what see we, but his station here,
From which to reason, or to which refer?
Thro' worlds unnumber'd tho' the God be known,
'Tis ours to trace him only in our own. Pope
IS
WS
Margaret Stockel. aged ten Years

Opposite: Early nineteenth century sampler by Margaret Stockel. The owners of the new villas were enthusiastic gardeners. Above: Mary Pether's sampler dated 1839 depicting a house and gardens with smooth lawns. J. C. Loudon's Suburban Gardener and Villa Companion *was addressed to the owners of such properties.*

which also appeared in 1841: "This fashionable tapestry work seems quite to have usurped the place of the various other embroideries which have from time to time engrossed the leisure moments of the fair."

The Countess described how Berlin patterns on squared paper with each tiny square representing a stitch were first imported at the beginning of the century. There was not a great deal of choice until Mr Wilks, the enterprising owner of Wilks' Warehouse in Regent Street in London, began importing patterns and the brilliant coloured "Zephyr" wools direct from Berlin. By 1840, 14,000 patterns had been published, only half of them even "moderately good" according to the Countess. The glare of colour was not to her taste, but though she realised the work might be considered mechanical she still found "infinitely more scope for fancy, taste and even genius" in this embroidery than in the "satin sketches" whose popularity had been eclipsed by the new craze. Few would agree with her view today, for these satin sketches left some room for personal choice in colours and stitchery whereas Berlin woolwork was about as individual as painting by numbers.

Exactly the same might be said about the geometrical flower gardens of the time in which not only the layout, but the choice of flowers and colours could be copied direct from a plan in a book or magazine. Whether such a plan was transferred to the garden or to canvas, the method was identical. Mrs Loudon wrote to help ladies whose enthusiasm for Berlin woolwork might exceed their knowledge of practical gardening. "It is scarcely possible to imagine any person more completely ignorant of everything related to botany and gardening that I was at the period of my marriage to Mr Loudon." But her ignorance was soon dispelled. She had married the most expert and prolific garden writer of his day, John Claudius

Loudon, and despite the fact that he was an "able and never wearied instructor" she must have felt some trepidation at the outset.

John Loudon's right arm had been amputated some years before his marriage, so as well as tending the vast range of plants in the garden of their house in Porchester Terrace, Bayswater, she took down the text of his books working with him late into the night. Jane Loudon, née Webb, was herself a successful writer and it was the reading of her eerie and thrilling novel *The Mummy* which prompted Loudon to make her acquaintance. In *Gardening for Ladies,* published in 1840, the first of her many books on the subject, she spread the knowledge she had acquired during ten years of hard work and study in a simple but direct and appealing manner. "The great point is to exercise our own skill and ingenuity; for we all feel so much more interested in what we do ourselves than in what is done for us, that no lady is likely to become fond of gardening who does not do a great deal with her own hands."

Title page of Mrs Loudon's Gardening for Ladies. *The information in her books was practical and easy to follow. On several occasions she compared gardening with embroidery to make a point clear.*

The book was exactly what the Victorian lady with an interest in flowers and plenty of time to spend on her garden needed. With the advent of the Industrial Revolution gardening, like embroidery, was no longer the exclusive preserve of the nobility and gentry. "Opulent commercial men," as Loudon referred to the newly rich middle classes, bought his book *The Suburban Gardener and Villa Companion* of 1836 for advice on embellishing their gardens, while their wives preferred Mrs Loudon's books which began to appear in the 1840's, as they were less formidable and easier to follow. Her advice was accurate, practical and clear, and imparted with such enthusiasm that the books remain as instructive and pleasurable as when they were written.

In her edition of *The Villa Companion* published in 1850, Mrs Loudon once again chose the comparison of embroidery to encourage her readers. "There is scarcely such a thing to be found as a lady who is not fond of flowers; but it is not saying too much to affirm that there are very few ladies indeed who are competent to lay out a flower garden; though the skill required to do so is within the capacity of every woman who can work or embroider patterns for the different parts of a female dress: and, supposing a female to have grown up without the slightest knowledge of the art of working a pattern, or tracing out a flower garden, it would certainly be much easier for her to acquire the latter art than the former."

In 1850 Mrs Loudon edited *The Ladies Companion*, a magazine with stories, poems and reviews as well as articles on embroidery and gardening. In some issues the "Work Basket" section lies adjacent to her articles on aspects of "The Garden" as if to suggest they were connected. In an article on the flower garden, Mrs Loudon explained the difference between a mixed and a geometrical flower garden, with plans and plant lists for the latter. "In a geometrical flower garden," she wrote, "the colours must be contrived to produce a striking effect contrasted with each other, and the plants must be so chosen as to be nearly of the same size, so that the garden when seen at a distance may have the effect of a Turkey carpet,"—or of Berlin woolwork whose patterns and colours were strikingly similar to those of the carpet bedding in the geometrical garden.

Carpet bedding first became popular in the early 1830's, just as Berlin patterns and wools became readily available at Wilks' Warehouse. The plants were laid out in patterns as complex as any in the earlier knots or parterres, but the effect was quite different because of the garish colours of the new bedding plants, many of them recently introduced exotics forced in hot houses during the winter. Joseph Paxton who designed the vast greenhouse—the Great Stove—for the Duke of Devonshire at Chatsworth was also one of the originators of the carpet bedding style.

"What is of chief interest about him," wrote Mrs Earle, a keen gardener and writer of the time, "is that he was the greatest unconscious instrument in the movement he helped to develop, which altered the gardening of the whole of England, and consequently of the world. He used the old patterns of Italy and France for designs of beds, filling them, as had never been done before, with cuttings of tender exotics, which were kept under glass during the whole winter."

Carpet bedding like Berlin woolwork persisted into the 1870's. In *The Amateur's Flower Garden* published in 1871 Shirley Hibberd, famous as the author of *Rustic Adornments for Homes of Taste*, described "leaf embroidery" bedding in which only foliage plants, or geraniums with their flowers picked off, were used and which was "equally well adapted to the grandest terrace garden or the quite humble and unpretending grass plot in a villa garden. It may be likened in a general way to a hearthrug or Turkey carpet pattern." Hibberd referred his readers to an article in the *Floral World* of March 1871 where this type of bedding was described in full. It bore "such general resemblance to embroidery as to justify the name by which this system is to be henceforth known. The

Top: The "Campana" Berlin woolwork design from The English Woman's Domestic Magazine. *Bottom: The White Sand Garden from* The Handy Book of the Flower Garden *by David Thomson. Both the design and the material look back to the earlier parterres.*

displays of embroidery in the subtropical garden at Battersea Park last season were so remarkably rich and tasteful, and as meritorious for originality of designs as for the splendour of the effect produced."

Leaf embroidery was designed to produce "sheets of colour", and its novelty lay in being slightly more muted than the effects of the previous decades. In the same book Hibberd also described "a curious and eminently pleasing style of massing known as tesselated colouring, the colours being repeated in small blotches with sharp dividing lines to separate the groups." This sounds very similar to the look of geometrical Berlin patterns in such periodicals as *The Young Ladies Journal* and *The English Woman's Domestic Magazine*.

The Victorians also brought back into fashion the parterre of box and coloured sands which had, as Shirley Hibberd said, the "advantage that, during winter, it affords something to look at, but the corresponding disadvantage that nobody wants to see it."

The connections between carpet bedding and Berlin woolwork remained remarkably close throughout the fifty years when both were in favour, and changes of fashion in flowers, colours and arrangement appeared in each of them simultaneously as if by some curious cross-fertilisation. The brightest possible colours were admired till the 1860's and 1870's when more muted shades were preferred, and the most complicated geometrical patterns for Berlin woolwork coincided with the most intricate effects in the garden. There were corresponding echoes too in the choice of flowers. In the 1830's the embroidered flowers, as bright as the colours on the patterns and the matching wools, often tended to be old favourites like roses, auriculas, pansies and poppies which were equally popular in the garden. But with the development of greenhouse culture, gaily coloured annuals and showy exotics joined these favourites which had themselves become

blowsy and inflated-looking as if in competition with the newcomers. Arum lilies and orchids were prized as much by needlewomen as by gardeners, and appeared in patterns and illustrations in magazines and books on both subjects.

In *The Ladies Country Companion* published in 1845, subtitled "How to Enjoy a Country Life Rationally," Mrs Loudon gave advice in a series of letters written to encourage Annie, a newly-married friend who had to give up town life for a home in the country

Opposite: Flowers in raised woolwork embroidered in brilliant Berlin wools to create domed effects as in carpet bedding.
Top: These domed effects are illustrated in "a bed of Picturesque Plants" from The Handy Book of the Flower Garden *by David Thomson. Bottom: Carpet bedding today in the gardens of Victoria Park in London where groups of plants are still "raised above the groundwork" in the Victorian manner.*

and was thoroughly miserable as a result. Annie's husband's house had a gloomy and neglected garden and Mrs Loudon explained precisely how she should improve matters by laying out a geometrical flower garden. This was soon accomplished and Mrs Loudon congratulated Annie on the effect: "now so brilliant with bright scarlet verbenas and golden yellow calceolarias that you can scarcely gaze at it in the sunshine."

This is one of Mrs Loudon's most delightful books, and her views on gardening often seem equally appropriate for embroidery. "Gardening," she wrote to Annie, "is one of those happy arts in which there is always some not quite certain change, to look forward to, and to be anxious about." Flowers as brilliant as those she described were further intensified in needlework by the contrast of a dark background. This set them off just as handsomely as the velvety lawns—now clipped smooth by

the revolutionary new mowing machine invented by Mr Budding—set off the vivid carpet bedding. The effect is charmingly described by Molly, the heroine of Mrs Gaskell's novel *Wives and Daughters*, published in 1864, when she visits her aristocratic neighbours at the Towers and is delighted by the sight of "green velvet lawns, bathed in sunshine . . . and flower beds too, scarlet, crimson, blue and orange; masses of blossom lying on the greensward." In the book Molly helps her father's gardener to plan some new flower beds, pegging them out in squares using Mrs Loudon's method. The old man is quite perplexed at first, but after further explanation declares, "All right, Miss Molly. I'se getten it in my head as clear as patchwork now."

A striking three-dimensional effect was achieved in Berlin woolwork using plush stitch to make a chosen motif stand out from the background. A similar stitch had been used in stumpwork to convey the roundness of woolly sheep or curving grassy slopes. With plush stitch the motifs could be contoured by the carefully graduated shearing of the loops of wool worked into the canvas. Soft textured birds, fruit, flowers and other details could be raised up to produce domed shapes rounded like the fashionable crinolines, like the flower beds in the gardens, and like the swelling aisles of the great greenhouses where the bedding plants were grown.

In *The Handy Book of the Flower Garden* which first appeared in 1868, David Thomson described similar shapes with plants rising in pyramidal, pincushion and shaded beds. He also recommended "panel planting" where groups of plants were also "slightly elevated above the groundwork." He was particularly impressed by the garden at Cleveland House in Clapham, where the beds were "ramped up by turf . . . and the surface has a very gentle rise towards the centre. In planting and finish they are perfect; and in colouring, brilliancy is combined with chasteness." Sixty thousand plants were used in this bedding scheme, most of them foliage plants, indicative of the change of fashion favouring less gaudy effects. The leaf embroidery of the 1870's corresponds with the more sombre shades used in the geometric designs of the last phase of Berlin woolwork; and as in the garden of Cleveland House "mathematical precision is the very essence of this decoration."

GARDENING WITH SILK AND GOLD THREAD

"A lovely pleasance,
set with flowers, foursquare."

William Morris *The Life and Death of Jason*

Unlike most of his contemporaries, William Morris turned his back on the strident colours and mechanical effects of carpet bedding and Berlin woolwork and created the pleasance of his poem in his own gardens and in his embroidery. He drew inspiration from happy childhood memories of days spent out of doors, and from the flowers and gardens of the distant mediaeval past which haunted his imagination and influenced all his art.

His first home, the Red House at Bexley Heath in Kent, was designed for him by his friend Philip Webb. The garden was laid out on the lines of a mediaeval pleasance. "In front of the house it was spaced formally into four little square gardens making a big square together; each of the smaller squares had a wattled fence around it with an opening by which one entered, and all over the fence roses grew thickly." In the illuminated manuscripts which he collected, Morris would have seen wattle fences of this kind and similar enclosures where the grass was powdered with flowers. When Morris and his wife Jane began furnishing the Red House, they could find little that appealed to them ready-made, and so Morris began to design what he needed himself. Jane provided him with some indigo-dyed blue serge and Morris began to work simple flowers on it in soft-coloured crewel wools, spacing them on the ground in the manner of a flowery mead. Jane helped in the embroidery and they used the hangings to cover the walls of the bedroom.

In 1882 in the *Lesser Arts of Life*, Morris declared, "to turn our chamber walls into the green woods of the leafy month of June, populous of bird and beast; or a summer garden with man and maid playing round a fountain; that surely was worth the trouble of doing, and the money that had to be paid for it."

As in the past, embroidery brought the garden indoors, and with it came echoes of a far-off world of romance and chivalry. For the dining room at the Red House, Morris designed a series of embroideries depicting Chaucer's "Illustrious Women." The graceful figures stand as if on the raised and flower-bedecked border of a

Frontispiece of The Wild Garden *by William Robinson with plants growing naturally, in total contrast to the schemes in the geometrical garden.*

mediaeval pleasance, and if all the series had been completed the effect in the room would surely have been that of a mysterious garden alive with legendary figures.

Embroidery, like the other arts, should "remind you of something beyond itself, of something of which it is a visible symbol." In his designs Morris wanted "unmistakeable suggestions of gardens and fields, and strange trees, boughs and tendrils.

Within the orderly framework of the garden, informal planting was the most desirable. The structure of individual plants and their growth—rising, expanding and unfurling—fascinated Morris and inspired his great swirling designs. Some of his contemporaries found the exuberant foliage overwhelming. Lady Marion Alford writing in *Needlework as Art* in 1886 described Morris's "repetition of vegetable forms" as being reminiscent of a "kitchen garden in a tornado."

His intimate knowledge of needlework as well as his genius for design made Morris well aware of the dangers of "cheap and commonplace naturalism." In a lecture he gave in 1881 on "Hints on Pattern Designing" he said: "It is a quite delightful idea to cover a piece of linen cloth with roses, jonquils and tulips done quite natural with the needle and we can't go too far in that direction if we only remember the needs of our material and the nature of our craft in general: these demand that our roses and the like, however unmistakeably roses, shall be quaint and naive to the last degree, and also that since we are using specially beautiful materials, that we shall make the most of them and not forget that we are gardening with silk and gold thread."

ART NEEDLEWORK AND THE WILD GARDEN

On a freezing night in the winter of 1861 a young gardener named William Robinson let out the fires in his employer's greenhouses, opened all the windows and exposed to the frost the entire collection of tropical plants which had been entrusted to him. He then packed his bags and left. Robinson had a hot temper and his callous action was probably the result of an argument with the head gardener or his employer, but it also summed up feelings he was later to express in his books about "the repulsively gaudy manner" in which vast quantities of greenhouse plants covered the ground in the bedding schemes of Victorian gardens.

Robinson's next job was far more to his taste. He was put in charge of a garden of English wild flowers in the Royal Botanical Society's garden in Regents Park. He went on trips in search of new flowers for the collection, and came to appreciate the beauty of hardy plants in their natural surroundings. Gradually he evolved the idea of a "wild garden" as an alternative to the regimented effects of carpet bedding. He described how to make a "charming little hardy garden, or series of beds filled with the better kinds of our native plants . . . and shrubs . . . surrounded with English trees" in a book published in 1870 and appropriately entitled *The Wild Garden, or Our Groves and Shrubberies Made Beautiful*.

Robinson's book was well timed, for the public were beginning to tire of the geometrical gardens and their garish colours and "some are looking back with regret, to the old mixed border gardens" with their "sweet old border flowers." These flowers and many wild ones too were listed by Robinson and they included lilies, bluebells, foxgloves, columbines, honeysuckle, daffodils, irises, wild roses and brambles. The list corresponds exactly with the flowers that were coming into favour in Art Needlework, suggesting that the embroiderer was as tired of garish Berlin woolwork as the gardener was with carpet bedding.

Art Needlework was to become as much of a craze as Berlin woolwork. Like William

Opposite: Victorian parterres where hothouse bedding plants were lavishly displayed, from E. A. Brooke's Gardens of England. *Below: Musicians in a garden setting in a panel designed by William Morris c 1875.*

Left: Geometric patterns in Berlin woolwork. Above: Geometric garden designs illustrating an article by Mrs Loudon in The Ladies Companion. *Mrs Loudon listed all the flowers to be used, indicating their place on the plan so that it could be followed as exactly as a pattern for Berlin woolwork. Opposite: "Unmistakeable suggestions of gardens" in the bed hangings at Kelmscott Manor embroidered by William Morris's daughter May. Morris's crewel wools were specially dyed to produce beautiful soft colours, sometimes using receipts from Fuchs' sixteenth century herbal to obtain the right shades. The harsh colours and mechanical effects of the geometrical gardens disgusted and saddened Morris. In "Hopes and Fears for Art" he referred to the current fashion as "an aberration of the human mind called carpet bedding," and he went on: "Need I explain further? I had rather not, for when I think of it, even when I am quite alone, I blush with shame at the thought." The hangings evoke the earlier pleasances and the gardens "well fenced from the outer world" which Morris enjoyed at Kelmscott.*

Opposite: Upper section of a panel designed and worked by William Morris. The swirling foliage with smaller motifs in the background recalls William Robinson's ideal of tall plants rising "in their own wild way" from a carpet of dwarf subjects. Above: Daisy and strawberry designs for cushion covers from Art Embroidery, *1878.*

Robinson searching out old varieties in undisturbed cottage gardens, enthusiasts of Art Needlework looked back to the embroidery of the past with renewed interest. In 1872 the Royal School of Art Needlework was founded, and here old embroideries were studied and repaired, and many old designs were copied and sold as patterns. The designs could be embroidered in outline in crewel wool or silk on linen, or filled in in imitation of the stitchery of seventeenth century patterns. These "Jacobean" designs were especially popular, and so were the flowers of the wild garden. They were used to powder the ground in embroidery, echoing "the meadow effect" advocated by Robinson, or spaced in simple borders like those he described in *The English Flower Garden* of 1883.

Elizabeth Glaister and M. S. Lockwood's criticism of the "gaudy obtrusiveness of the Berlin wool flower groups" in *Art Embroidery* in 1878 echoes Robinson's diatribes against bedding plants. "We can no longer be satisfied with filling up little squares or diamonds ready traced in certain fixed colours on canvas specially prepared," they wrote, and in the chapter "On Design" they suggested an alternative: "Taking for granted that flowers and leaves are the most suitable subjects for embroidery, we shall find that the simplest flowers are the best, as they are those which can be most fully expressed by the fewest lines, if in outline, and with the fewest shades of colours. It will be obvious that double flowers are unsuitable; we must be content with wild roses . . . and old fashioned flowers."

The colour harmonies in Art Needlework were to reflect those of nature, and Elizabeth Glaister recommended that her readers take the Berlin wools out into a sunlit garden and compare their discordant hues with the tones of real flowers.

The pioneer of the new style was William Morris whose designs had been available from his own firm, Morris, Marshall, Faulkner and Company, since its opening in 1861, and from the Royal School of Needlework. The subtle colours of the foliage in Morris's early designs were echoed in the gardeners' first attempts to "soften the harshness of the bedding system by the introduction of fine leaved plants" noted by Robinson in *The Wild Garden.* Morris's designs for vigorous plants surging up through smaller daintier flowers appear to be following Robinson's rule "never to show the naked earth but to carpet it with dwarf subjects, then allow taller ones to rise in their own wild way through the turf."

In practice the wild garden needed to be as carefully planned as a Morris design, and there could be nothing haphazard

about the arrangement of the plants. Without such thought, attempts at wild gardening often resulted in a rather piecemeal collection of hardy plants, just as a profusion of Art Needlework flowers "on pieces of linen hung over the furniture", merely recalled "a washing day" in Elizabeth Glaister's opinion. What was needed was considerable skill in the arrangement of the chosen flowers to suit the setting, and this advice soon appeared in the books of Miss Gertrude Jekyll.

JAPONAISERIE

"In a subtle, mysterious way the mystic spell of the flowery land has been cast over our English Gardens. This spell has touched the quiet slumbering beauty of the Old English Garden, and with its fairy wand has transformed it into a living picture. All the magic and witchery of the East are apparent, and under its influence the English Garden is entering upon halcyon days, and where we once had to look deep for beauty, lo! here we are confronted by it at every turn. Certainly, the outcome of this blending of East with West will make for daintiness and simplicity in the garden, and, furthermore, it has completely widened the scope of the landscape gardener."

This extract from the *Gardener's Magazine* was quoted in the "special items" section of V. N. Gauntlett and Company's garden catalogue at the beginning of this century, under the title *Japanese Art in English Gardens*. The firm advertised all the "special items" necessary to create such a "living picture"—Japanese maples "to light up the whole landscape"; dainty tea houses clad with wondrous coverings of wistaria; flowering trees and shrubs such as magnolias, cherries, and azaleas which are "ousting the funereal Cypress, and other heavy evergreens our fathers loved to plant," and the "Japanese Ideal in Stonework" in the shape of "interesting old Stone seats, exquisite Stone Bridges and charming Stone Lanterns which at nightfall shed their diffused rays over rippling pools and waving irises."

The writer in the *Gardener's Magazine* is describing a garden in the Japonaiserie style which had first appeared in England in the 1860's when it seemed as novel and exciting as Chinoiserie once had been—and as far removed from reality.

As had happened when Chinoiserie became popular in the late seventeenth century "the most obvious and superficial qualities of Japanese art" were seized on by embroiderers and other artists and craftsmen. The complex symbolism of Japanese flowers and gardens remained a mystery to most people, and although some enthusiasts brought Japanese experts to England to lay out authentic designs, most gardeners relied on magazines and books like Josiah Conder's *Landscape Gardening in Japan* written in 1893, in which they could see illustrated all the Eastern trappings now available from the nurserymen.

The embroiderer could buy Japonaiserie designs or use separate motifs to arrange as she liked when creating her own impression of a Japanese garden. Elizabeth Glaister described the kind of designs available for screens in *Needlework* published in 1880 where "each panel is a kind of suggestive picture. The more solid plants grow up from the ground, or out of very conventional water; higher up a bird flies across, or perches, and is balanced by a suggestion of a cloud or a projecting spray of flowers."

Not only Japanese gardens but Japanese embroideries could now be copied, and examples of the latter reached the London sale rooms in the 1870's. Their complexities, like the finer points of Japanese gardens, were usually disregarded as Elizabeth Glaister remarked in 1878, in *Art Embroidery:* "The beauties of Japanese Needlework are, like those of other art work from that wonderful land very far from being rightly understood here by more than a few; and though a wave of fashion has swept numberless objects of Japanese art into this country their real merits are as yet but little appreciated."

One designer who did appreciate them was Thomas Jekyll, whose design of cranes worked as a hanging in silks and crewel wools on cotton sheeting was exhibited twice in the 1870's, first in America at the Philadelphia Centennial Exhibition in 1876, and then two years later in Paris at the Universal Exhibition. The birds and their setting of flowers and foliage have been worked to show off the structure both of the feathers and the leaves, and in this they are faithful to Japanese embroidery whose "fineness, firmness and precision of workmanship" Walter Crane so much admired.

As adapted by European embroiderers the designs were most effective on large scale hangings and screens, but small motifs were also popular for decorating less ambitious items, including irregularly shaped pieces of crazy patchwork. Perhaps William Morris had these particularly in mind when he wrote an article on textiles in the catalogue of the first Arts and Crafts Exhibition in London in 1888. Here he stressed the importance of beautiful materials in embroidery. His own ideas on "gardening with silk and gold thread" were simple in comparison with the sophistication of Japanese embroidery, and he warned "those occupied in embroidery" against "the feeble imitations of Japanese art that are so disastrously common among us. The Japanese are admirable naturalists, wonderful skilful draughtsmen, deft beyond all others in mere execution of whatever they take in hand . . . But with all this a Japanese design is absolutely worthless unless it is executed with Japanese skill." It was advice which gardeners and embroiderers seldom took sufficiently to heart, though their attempts to recreate Japanese gardens went on into the first decades of the twentieth century.

Opposite: Detail from a wall hanging by Thomas Jekyll in silks and wools on cotton sheeting. Right above: Jizo-In Mibu from Josiah Conder's Landscape Gardening in Japan. *Right below: "Water lily tank in our Nursery," photograph from V. N. Gauntlett's catalogue of 1901 illustrating some of the "special items" such as cranes in bronze, designed to add "mystic influence" to the scene.*

MODERN GARDENS

Steps into a delightful unknown

Gertrude Jekyll

THE INFLUENCE
OF GERTRUDE JEKYLL

Like Mrs Delany in the eighteenth century Gertrude Jekyll in more recent times thought of herself as a "working amateur." Her interests embraced nearly all the concerns of this book. She was deeply involved with plants, garden design and with needlework. In the realm of garden design, she has been the most important influence since William Robinson. She knew William Morris and was a friend of Robinson and shared many of their convictions.

The ideal of the designer-craftsman appealed to her strongly and like Morris, she combined talent for design with practical experience of the many crafts which interested her. In middle age her eyesight failed, cutting her off from painting and embroidery, and she directed her creative talents to garden design and writing.

Her many books remain an inspiration and a delight to read, and her views have shaped garden design throughout this century. They hold a particular fascination for those who share a dual interest in gardens and embroidery, as many of her remarks on gardens especially concerning colour and design are equally apt when applied to embroidery.

In *Home and Garden* written in 1926, she described the interior of Munstead Wood, the house designed for her by her friend and associate, the young Edward Lutyens. In these descriptions she reveals her feelings about embroidery. On her travels, she collected embroideries of all kinds both old and new. Some were displayed in the house, while most were preserved in "handy dark green boxes in deep panelled cupboards," together with her own materials—Algerian and other embroidery silks, crewel wools, chenille and coloured cottons and linens, and silks and cottons for working on.

"From time to time many of the materials come into use, while the rest are for the pleasure of turning over myself and showing to friends of like tastes and about it all is the comfortable feeling that everything is kept clean and safe and easily accessible." Her words suggest that she was on the same closely intimate and friendly terms with the materials of embroidery as she was with the plants she loved. Her cupboards, made with the same loving craftsmanship as everything else in the house, recall John Rea's seventeenth century "cabinet" garden with its precious contents.

At Munstead Wood, there was a large table where "needlework is cut out and arranged." In the 1870's, her diary records that she was at work on a cushion with dandelion, mistletoe, pomegranate and strawberry. Sadly, her needlework, like Mrs Delany's, has been dispersed, but it was obviously beautiful both in technique and design. Lord Leighton saw some of her work on linen and serge at an exhibition and so much admired their "remarkable merit in point of colour and arrangement" that he commissioned a tablecover for his dining room. Her own designs can be seen in L. Higgin's *Handbook of Embroidery*, published in 1880, which included borders by the illustrator Walter Crane and a hanging by William Morris.

Miss Jekyll's garden designs, carefully planned out on paper with horizontal drifts of plants merging one into another, were arranged to "form beautiful pictures." She believed it essential to "place every plant or group of plants with such thoughtful care and definite intention that they shall form part of a harmonious whole, and that successive portions, or in some cases even single details, shall show a series of pictures."

This extract is taken from *Colour Schemes for the Flower Garden* which of all her books is the most enlightening and stimulating for embroiderers. She shared William Robinson's deep love of plants, but she had a greater understanding of how best to use them to create beautiful pictures, and she warned her readers of the pitfalls of natural gardening. Ill-assorted plants in the garden were no better than paints set out on a palette, or a worthless library "made up of single volumes when there should be complete sets. Given the same space of ground and the same materials they may be fashioned either into a dream of beauty, a place of perfect rest and

Picture embroidered in coloured silks by Mrs Ethel Berners-Wilson c 1930. Both the plant associations and colour scheme suggest the influence of Gertrude Jekyll. Iris were among the waterside plants she recommended in Wall and Water Gardens.

Collection of The Hon. Mrs Edward Cust

refreshment of minds . . . or they may be so misused that everything is jarring and displeasing."

Jarring effects were most likely to result when too many plants were used and Miss Jekyll warned against the temptation of acquiring plants without a clear idea of how they were to be arranged. Her herbaceous borders were famous for their profusion, but this effect was achieved by rigorous restraint in the choice of each plant to enhance the tones, forms and textures of its neighbours. Her groups were always generous, thus avoiding the "shopwindow" or "washing day" effect which led the plantsman E. A. Bowles to criticise "the school of gardening that encourages the selection of plants merely as artistic furniture chosen for colour only like ribbons or embroidery silk."

It was true that Miss Jekyll's use of colour made her gardens unique, but she was equally concerned with the setting and with the qualities of the plants involved and how best to combine them to realize the effect she had in mind. One imagines her at the table at Munstead Wood assembling her embroidery materials and considering the role they were to play in the whole design which would be as far removed from mere "artistic furniture" as her sensitive garden pictures. "Whether the arrangement is simple or modest, whether it is bold or gorgeous, whether it is obvious or whether it is subtle, the aim is always to use the plants to the best of one's means and intelligence to form pictures of living beauty."

Top: Design for a "garden of summer flowers" with the plants arranged in generous horizontal drifts from Gertrude Jekyll's Colour Schemes for the Flower Garden. *Bottom: Embroidery designs of periwinkle and iris by Gertrude Jekyll illustrated in L. Higgin's* Handbook of Embroidery.

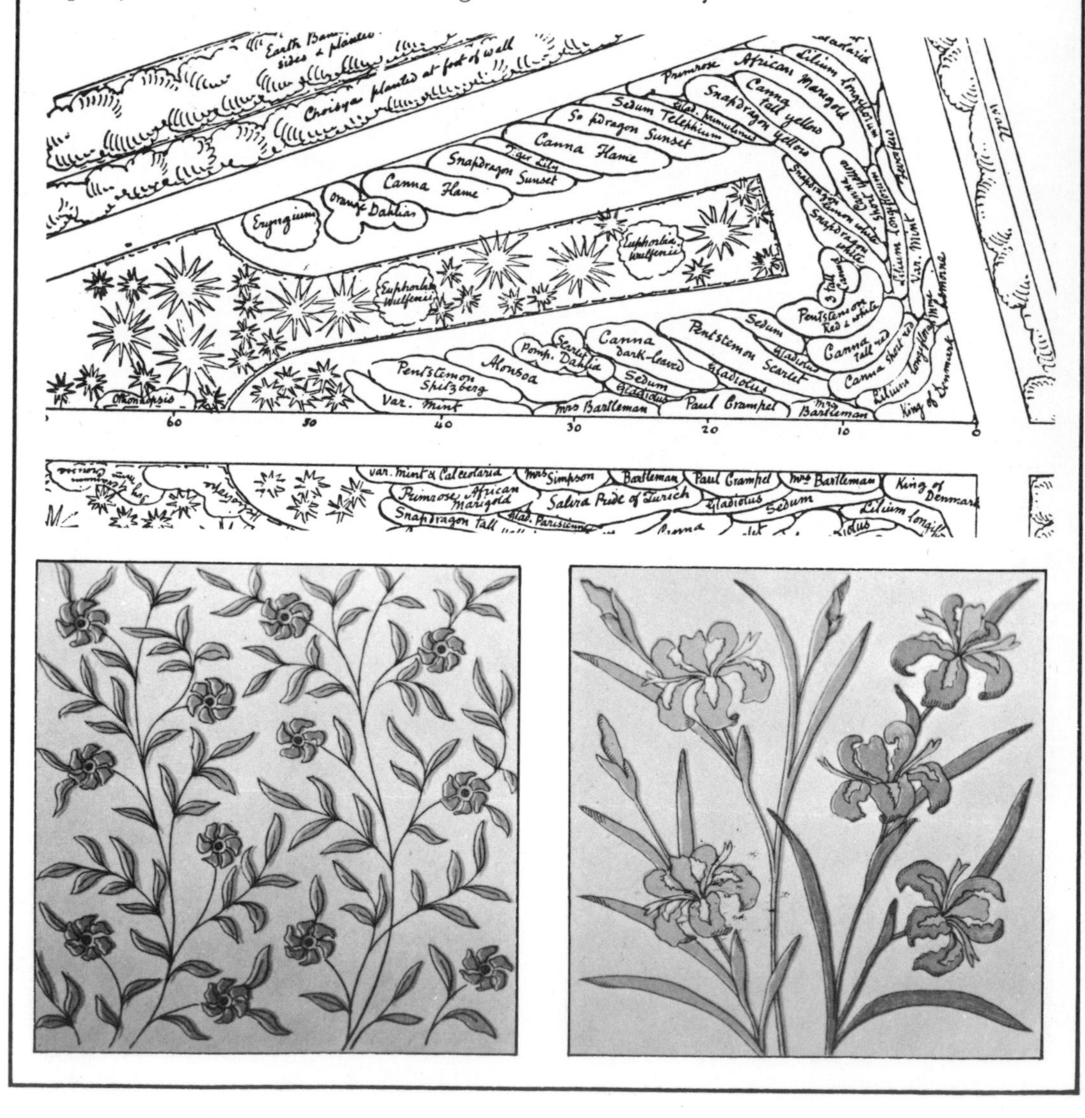

To this end she cultivated a trained colour eye which enabled her to "use colour to the best garden effects." She called it a kind of optical gastronomy, this kind of preparation and presentation of food for the eye in which each course is so designed that it is the best possible preparation for the ones to come. This optical gastronomy is best appreciated in "Gardens of Special Colouring", blue, grey, gold or green, the forerunners of the grey and white gardens of today, or patios where foliage plants make refreshing green pictures within a small compass. As always, Gertrude Jekyll combined common sense with artistic knowledge and a sense of beauty and she reminded her readers that including flowers just because they were "grey" or "blue" was not the only criterion. "Any experienced colourist knows that the blues will be more telling—more purely blue—by the rightly placed complementary colour."

Knowing where to place the right shade of the complementary colour and how much to use, comes only with long experience and understanding of plants and Gertrude Jekyll never minimized the difficulties. She spent half her life contriving ways of achieving beauty and harmony in the garden, but when she looked back, she could remember no part of it that was not full of pleasure and encouragement. "For the love of gardening is a seed that once sown never dies, but always grows and grows to an enduring and ever-increasing source of happiness."

"The Old Playhouse" from Children and Gardens *by Gertrude Jekyll. The idea of a book to encourage young gardeners was suggested by her friend the architect Edward Lutyens. The broad leaved acanthus in the foreground contrasting with the more delicate foliage on the left are typical of Gertrude Jekyll's sensitive handling of plants.*

CHILDREN AND GARDENS

Echoes of garden pictures and patterns in twentieth century embroidery are fainter than before, or perhaps we are too close in time to perceive them. One charming connection noticeable at the turn of the century can be traced in the theme of children and gardens. It reflects a nostalgia for the innocence of childhood also apparent in contemporary paintings, books and book illustration. Many books ostensibly for children were also enjoyed by adults, and some of the best loved—as we have already seen in *Alice in Wonderland*—were concerned with children and gardens. Mrs Molesworth's *The Palace in the Garden* published in 1877, tells of mysterious presents which appear in a garden. Juliana Horatia Ewing's *Mary's Meadow* of 1886 is about a family of children who find John Parkinson's *Paradisus* in their father's library and make up the "Game of the Earthly Paradise," during which Mary replants the old-fashioned double cowslip in the meadow of the title. Included in the book were *Letters from a Little Garden* which contained practical gardening advice. In 1911 Frances Hodgson Burnett wrote *The Secret Garden* and here again the hero discovers the pleasures of gardening and the special atmosphere of secluded gardens.

Two other books were concerned entirely with the practical aspects of children's gardens. Mrs Loudon wrote the *Young Gardener's Year Book* in 1855, and her advice that children's gardens should be given a "nice sunny open air situation" was repeated by Miss Jekyll in *Children and Gardens* in 1911, when she implored parents not to offer some "unattractive out of the way corner" which would lead to failure and discouragement.

Both authors were perfectly in sympathy with their young readers' needs; their own enthusiasm shines through the information they provide and, in Miss Jekyll's case, it is linked with the most engaging humour. Here she is introducing herself at the start of her book. "Well do I remember the time when I thought there were two kinds of people in the world—children and grown ups—and that the world really belonged to children. And I think it is because I have been more or less a child all my life, that I still feel like a child in many ways although from the number of years I have lived I ought to know that I am quite an old woman." She was sixty-five at the time. She looks back to her own childhood and tells how she made daisy chains in Berkeley Square and was "attracted by dandelions" in Green Park. She and her sister had adjoining gardens with box-edged borders, laid out between the shrubbery of her parents' garden and a field. She wanted children to have a playhouse in the garden and she illustrates this idea with a plan and a photograph of "a pretty lady" sitting outside a playhouse "trying to think herself a child again."

The scene is reminiscent of the panel embroidered by Mary Newill around 1900, when she was teaching embroidery at the Birmingham School of Art. The two children are enjoying picking wild flowers in the grass outside their little garden. The flowers, like those in the roundel shown on page 118, worked at about the same date are bright and fresh in comparison with the muted tones of Art Needlework, as if the embroiderers had been influenced by the garden enthusiast J. D. Sedding who deplored the excessive reliance on the embroidery of the past, and encouraged the study of plants in the garden or in the wild. Mary Newill's panel is close to the spirit of the *Secret Garden*. " 'I wouldn't want it to look like a gardener's Garden all clipped and spick and span, would you?' he said. 'It's nicer like this with things running wild' . . . " These sentiments were most strongly held by Gertrude Jekyll who was "perpetually at amicable war with the gardener for over trimmers."

Miss Jekyll liked profusion and natural effects in the planting to be controlled by a skilful yet unobtrusive plan. As a child, she had a garden with yew hedges, frontiers of a private land, like the hedged enclosure on page 120 embroidered about 1910 where a girl is picking blossom, absorbed in a romantic world of her own, echoing once again the atmosphere of the *Secret Garden:* "It's a queer, pretty place. It's like as if a body was in a dream."

Panel by Mary Newill. "The garden should be something without and beyond nature; a page from an old romance, a scene in fairyland, a gateway through which the imagination lifted above the sombre realities of life may pass into a world of dreams." Sir George Sitwell, On The Making of Gardens, *1909. Far left: Handscreen "Mary, Mary Quite Contrary" embroidered by Catherine Powell in coloured silks.*

Opposite: Roundel of a child picking flowers c 1910.

"Innumerable the small flowers that stitch,
Their needlework of canvas on the ground."
V. Sackville West, The Garden

Above: Kew Gardens by Enid Deakin illustrated in the Studio Special Publication on Modern Embroidery *by Mary Hogarth. Enid Deakin used her own sketch for the design as recommended by Mary Hogarth in the introduction to the book. She approached the subject quite differently from the eighteenth century embroiderer whose picture of Kew shown on page 84 was copied from a print recalling the gentle rural pleasures of the time.*

The garden of childhood is carefree and mysterious, in tune with the naive yet appealing scenes embroidered in earlier centuries. A handscreen illustrating the nursery rhyme "Mary Mary quite Contrary" looks back to the topiary hedges and pebble-edged beds of Tudor and Stuart gardens, and the silver bells of Chinoiserie, but treats them prettily if sentimentally to suit contemporary taste. Whether they were children or adults, embroiderers of the past often chose a child's eye view of the garden, and these twentieth century embroideries continue the tradition.

SPRING

ANYTHING GOES

Gardens at the turn of the century were more eclectic in design than ever before. Some designers looked back to the gardens of the Renaissance and the seventeenth century, others continued to explore the possibilities of wild, rock and water gardens. Some, like Lawrence Johnston at Hidcote in Gloucestershire began to combine formal and informal elements successfully within a single garden. Here a varied series of enclosures differing in scale and character looks back to Sir William Temple's ideal arrangement of "rooms out of which you step into another." These are contrasted with areas treated as wild gardens. Johnston used trees, shrubs and flowers from all over the world whose qualities and contrasts would have enthralled earlier plant lovers. The modernity of Hidcote and other gardens laid out on similar lines, like Sissinghurst in Kent, lies in the imaginative use of this great wealth of plants.

Hidcote was laid out on a scale which is unthinkable today. Since the 1930's gardens, with a few rare exceptions, have been made on a far smaller scale, but though space, time and labour are more restricted than ever before, the interest and pleasure in gardens is undiminished. The idea expressed over three hundred years ago by the herbalist William Coles that "a house though otherwise beautiful, if it hath no Garden belonging to it is more like a Prison than a House" is as true today as it was then.

The wheel has come full circle and the well-designed small garden is now as closely related to the house as it was in the sixteenth century. As it is constantly seen from the house its winter appearance is carefully considered and in summer it is enjoyed for its privacy as a valuable extension to the house. The current fashion for light cane and bamboo furniture and numerous house plants once again brings the garden into the house, and embroidery continues to recreate the pictures and patterns of the garden for enjoyment indoors.

Gardens can be formal, informal or a little of both. Among the beds and borders, whether regular or irregular, there are likely to be some free shapes and forms. Embroidery reflects the interest in plant associations which is one of the most

Opposite: A girl picking blossoms c 1910. Contemporary children's books emphasized the private and mysterious nature of the garden. Below: Panel by Lillian Delevoryas. The interest in contrasting shapes, textures and tones is characteristic of modern gardens and embroidery.

Designed and made by Lillian Delevoryas

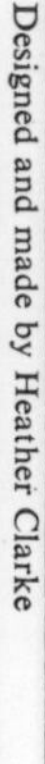

Designed and made by Heather Clarke

Designed and made by Audrey Walker

Three recent embroideries. Left: "Into the Garden" by Audrey Walker. Knots and seeding on cream canvas sprayed with dye. Above: "Formal Garden" by Heather Clarke, worked in a variety of techniques, including raised work and appliqué. Opposite: Machine embroidery on painted linen by the author, evoking the patterns in her knot garden in Dorset.

noticeable characteristics of modern gardens; textures, shapes and tones are as important to the embroiderer as to the gardener. The embroiderer may use a group of plants to suggest the quality of the whole garden, just as once she used vignettes of urns or pagodas to evoke the landscape garden.

In the early 1930's Enid Deakin sketched a group of trees in Kew Gardens and translated their shapes and tones into simple stitchery. Her picture was illustrated in the Studio Special Publication of 1933 on *Modern Embroidery* by Mary Hogarth and they exemplify the author's views. A painter herself, Mary Hogarth encouraged her contemporaries to be inventors and artists rather than imitators.

Like Jane Loudon a century earlier, she drew a parallel between designing for embroidery and for the garden to make the process appear less daunting. Answer-

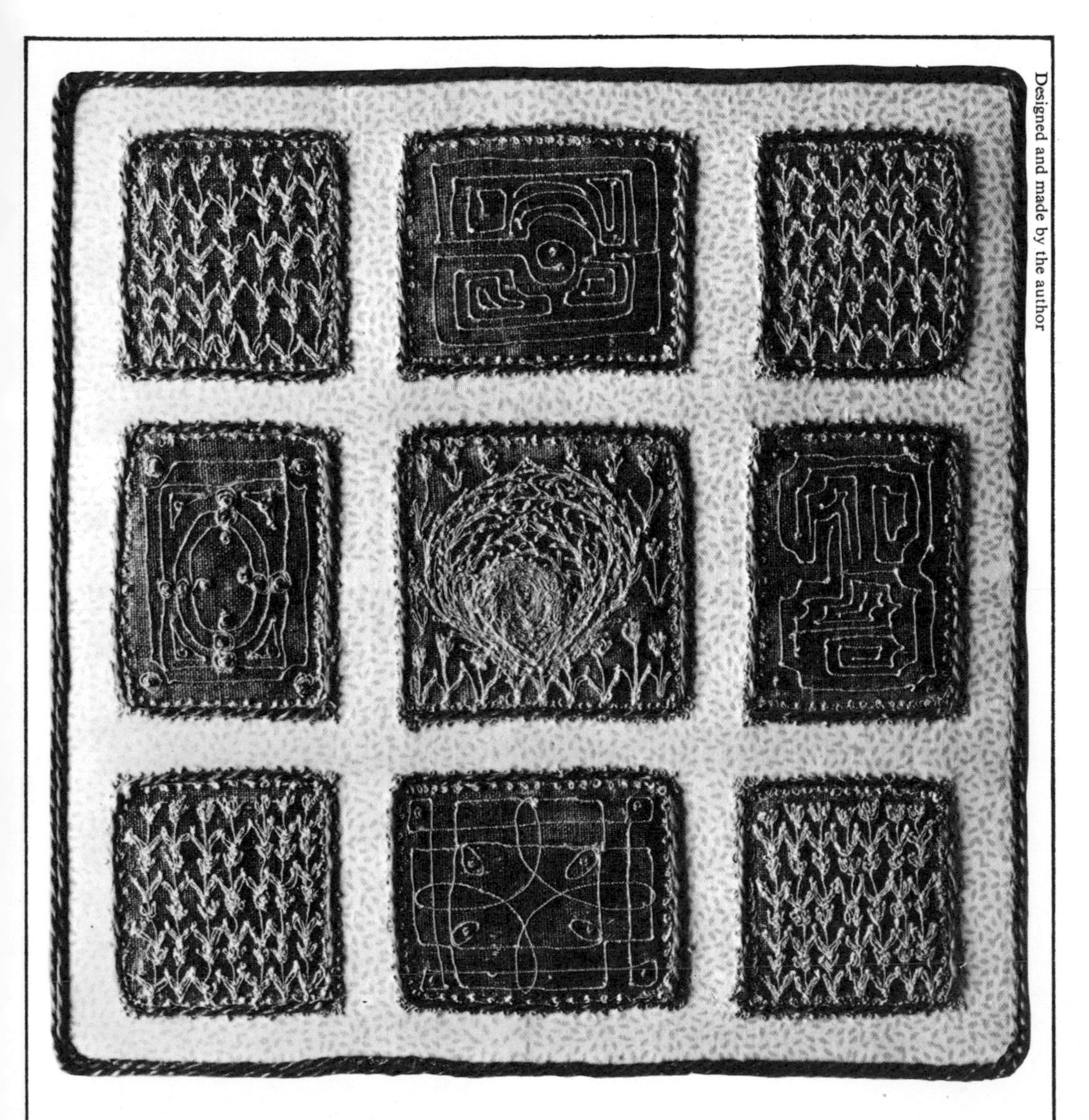

Designed and made by the author

ing the question, "Can we all design?" she replied "Yes, I think we can. Begin simply and you will be surprised how quickly it grows. We do design, we arrange all of us every day something, either our rooms, our gardens, our flowers. The counsel of perfection is to build up the design by stages on the material, and for the worker and designer to be one and the same person." Today we might use a sewing machine to fill in the outlines of our plants, chosen for their foliage as much as for their flowers, and have our garden complete in the time it would take to collect the plants from a garden centre and arrange them in their places. The picture we have at the end of the day will still depend on the design, but the means of achieving it will have been speeded up.

Sewing machines and all kinds of labour saving garden devices from mowers to weed killers are valuable time savers. They open up new horizons in terms of what can be undertaken. Ambitious hangings or the clipped hedges of a formal layout are once more within our reach. An idea sparked off by something seen in a garden, a museum, an exhibition becomes a possibility rather than a dream. We might have time for it. Embroidery with a machine is, however, as different from embroidering by hand as clipping a topiary specimen with hand shears is from using electric clippers. For both embroiderers and gardeners, the process—whether by machine or by hand—is as rewarding as the initial planning or the completed work.

When we make an embroidered garden today, the choice of pictures, patterns and plants is wider than ever before. Whatever we decide on, our creations will still reflect our pleasure in our own gardens and these embroideries may survive long after the much loved gardens have gone.

IDEAS FOR EMBROIDERING GARDENS

Materials and techniques

ENLARGING AND REDUCING DESIGNS

It is a simple matter to enlarge or reduce any design. Using this two-step method, you can copy and use any of the motifs in the book in any size you require for your own embroideries. First make a tracing of the chosen design. Then draw four lines, enclosing the whole design in a square or rectangular box. Divide the box into quarters and then divide again, and again until the whole design is covered by a grid of small even squares.

Draw a second box to the size you want the finished design to be. Divide this box into quarters and then divide again and again until there are exactly the same number of squares in the second box as in the first. All the squares in the second box will be proportionately larger or smaller than those in the first box. Transfer the design square by square from the first grid to the second. It will help you to keep track of the squares if you label them down the side and along the top with numbers and letters.

TRANSFERRING DESIGNS TO FABRIC

There are many ways of transferring an embroidery design to fabric. Three easy and versatile methods are shown here.

PRICK AND POUNCE
Trace the design onto fairly heavy paper. Place a folded sheet or felt pad on a firm surface, lay a sheet of tracing paper over the felt and place the tracing on top. Pin or tape the two sheets of paper together. You must now prick closely all around the outlines of the design. You can make a good tool to do this by breaking a needle in half and with a pair of pliers, pushing the blunt end into a pencil eraser. Work to a steady rhythm, spacing the holes evenly and closely. Go carefully around the details to ensure accurate reproduction. Tape the embroidery fabric to a firm surface, pin the perforated tracing paper on top. You will need some powdered charcoal (the pounce) and a pad of rolled and stitched felt or a blackboard eraser. Using a small amount of pounce at a time, rub it into the holes working the felt pad gently in a circular motion. Lift an edge of the tracing paper from time to time to check that the design is transferring well. Remove the tracing paper when you have finished the whole design.
Take a fine brush and some blue watercolour and paint the outlines of the design with a fine line. Begin with the edge nearest you, covering the line you have painted with a sheet of tissue paper so as not to smudge the pounce. When the paint is dry, flick the fabric hard to remove the pounce. Do not rub or it will smudge. On darker fabric, use powdered chalk for pounce and paint with white watercolour.

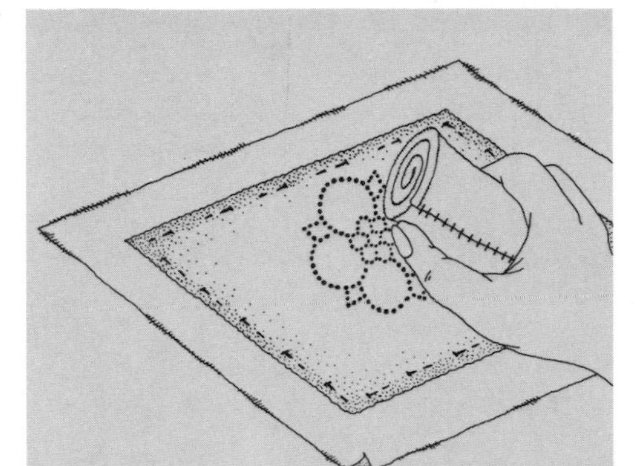

Far left: With the prick and pounce method, you can reproduce any design, however detailed.

Left: Rub the pounce in a little at a time using a circular motion. You will soon be able to gauge how much to use and how much pressure to apply.

TRACE AND BASTE
This method works best if you first mount the fabric in a frame. It is ideal for delicate fabrics, or for transferring a curving outline in counted thread embroidery.
Trace the motif on fine tissue paper. Place the paper on the fabric and pin in place—then baste the paper in position. With small running stitches sew all around the design through both paper and fabric. Remove the basting stitches around the edge and then tear the tissue paper away leaving the design outlined with stitches.

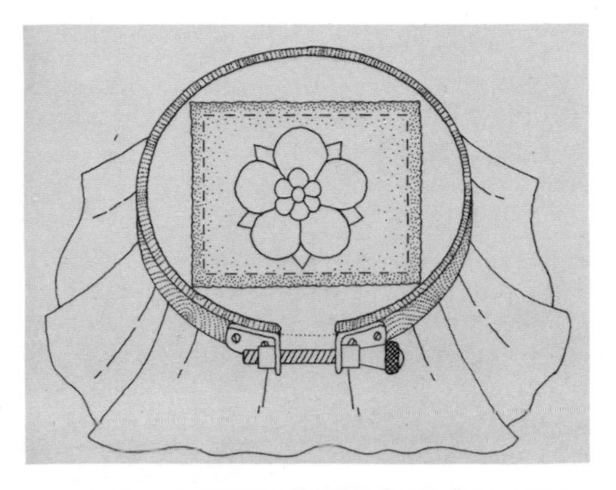

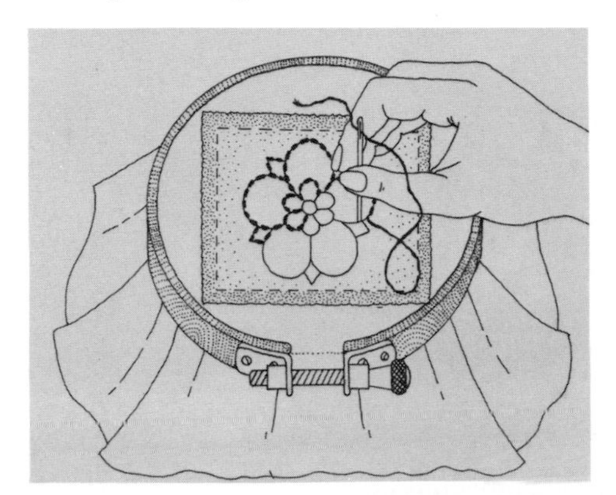

Far left: Baste a tracing of the motif to the fabric which has been stretched taut in a frame.

Left: Outline the design with small running stitches, sewing through both tracing paper and fabric.

THREADING A NEEDLE
You cannot thread a needle with wool using the standard method, so use this simple technique. Wrap the wool around the eye of the needle as shown and pull tightly.
Holding the wool close to the fold, slip it off the needle and push it through the eye.

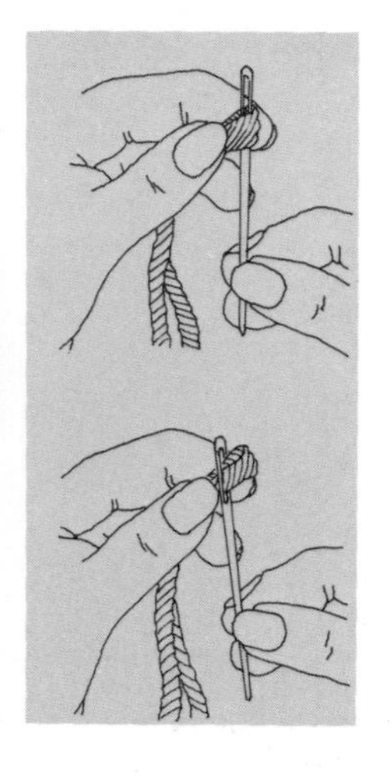

TRACE AND PAINT

Use this method to transfer designs to canvas. Trace the design with a bold, dark outline. Lay the tracing on a firm, white surface and place the canvas to be embroidered on top. Tape tracing and canvas in place on the surface. The design should show clearly through the canvas. You must use a waterproof paint or an indelible marker, to draw the design on the canvas.

FRAMES

Embroidery frames hold the background fabric firm and taut. They prevent the fabric from puckering during working and keep the grain of the fabric straight. A frame is useful though not essential when you are working counted thread embroidery as it helps to make the work even. Frames are also useful for working stitches which are formed in more than one movement. You must use a frame for working stumpwork, appliqué and couching as all these techniques must be worked with the background fabric taut and flat and they require the use of both hands.
There are two basic kinds of frame: round or tambour, and square or slate. Both kinds can be bought with floor stands or table stands which are useful as they leave both hands free. However, you can only work in the place where you have set up the frame; without a stand, an embroidery frame can travel about with you from place to place.

ROUND FRAMES

Round or tambour frames consist of two wooden rings. The outer ring fits over the inner and is tightened by a screw. To mount the fabric, first bind bias tape over the inner ring. This prevents the fabric from slipping and also prevents the frame from marking the fabric. Lay the fabric over the inner ring and push the outer ring over the top. Tighten the screw, making sure that this does not pull the weave of the fabric out of square. Do not use a round frame for working raised embroidery unless the circumference of the frame is larger than the area of the embroidery.

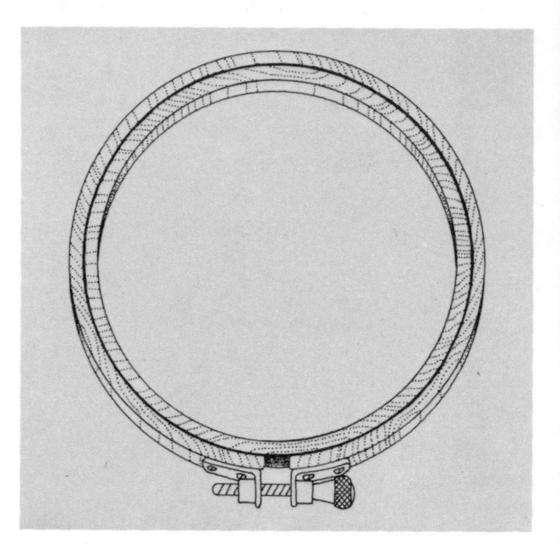

SQUARE FRAMES

The width of the canvas or fabric should not be greater than the width of the webbing attached to the rollers at top and bottom. The fabric may be of any length as the excess can be wound around the rollers. With an indelible marker, mark the centre of the webbing. Sew tape along the sides of the fabric and turn under a hem at top and botton. Mark the centre of the hems and sew the fabric to the webbing, matching the centres and working outwards from the centre each time. Wind any excess fabric around the rollers, insert the stretchers and adjust the tension. To maintain an overall tension, the fabric must be laced to the frame at the sides. Use a ball of thin string, and starting at one end, lace through the tape and around the stretchers. When you have laced one side, wind the string around the peg. Lace the other side. Tighten the laces and wind the excess around the pegs.

BLACKWORK

Blackwork is worked in a single colour, over counted threads of the background fabric or in a speckling technique.

FABRIC
Use cotton, linen or wool with evenly spaced threads. The fabric should be finely woven with from 30 to 18 threads to the inch (60 to 32 threads to 5 cm).

THREADS
Much of the beauty of blackwork depends on the weight and density of the patterns and the contrast between the intricate, lacy patterns and the plain background. You can use a variety of threads, but they should all be smooth. Hairy or fuzzy yarns blur the crisp outlines of the patterns and lessen the contrast between embroidery and background. Stranded embroidery thread is very versatile as you can use one or two strands for fine filling patterns on coarser fabric, or for outlines. Sewing silk and Coton à Broder are also suitable for filling patterns. For coarser work and for outlining, pearl cotton and soft embroidery cotton can be used.

NEEDLES
Use a blunt-ended tapestry needle which will go between the threads of the background fabric without splitting them. Sizes 18 to 26, which is the finest size, provide a good range for use with a variety of threads. In many blackwork designs, the geometric filling patterns are enclosed in a curving outline, for example within a vine or a leaf. To work these curving outlines, you will need a sharp-pointed crewel needle. Sizes from 1, the largest, to 7 are all suitable.

TRANSFERRING DESIGNS
Transfer any curving outlines using the trace and baste method which is described on page 125.

FRAMES
Either round or slate frames can be used for blackwork, as holding the work in a frame will help to produce more even stitches. See page 126 for information about frames.

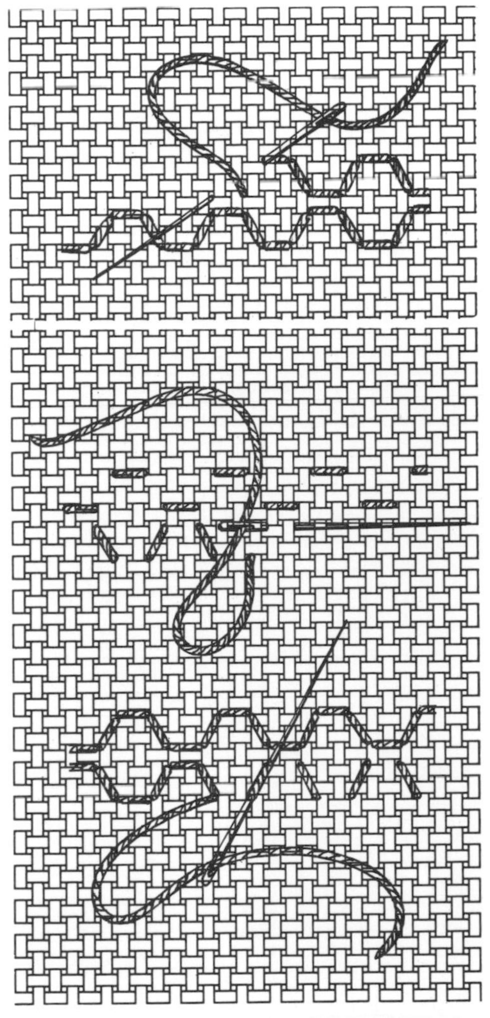

Blackwork uses only simple, basic stitches, but they must be worked accurately to produce regular and even patterns.

BACK STITCH
Keep all the stitches the same size and insert the needle into the same hole as the previous stitch.

DOUBLE RUNNING OR HOLBEIN STITCH
Work along the line of the design, covering every two alternate threads of the ground. Turn the work round and work back, filling in the spaces between the first line of running stitches. Insert the needle into the same holes as on the first line for a smooth continuous outline.

A late sixteenth century coif embroidered with a blackwork design of twining vines. Each leaf and each flower petal is worked with a different filling pattern.

PATTERN DARNING
This versatile filling stitch is composed simply of running stitches worked over a varying number of threads to create a pattern.

SPECKLING
Speckling is composed of small satin stitches worked close together and at random. It is not worked over counted threads.
Work a small stitch and then place a second over it in the same direction to form a single, slightly raised stitch. Speckling stitches can be worked close together to create a subtle, shaded effect.

Far right: These motifs can be filled with speckling, used small and repeated as filling patterns, or enlarged and used as design outlines to be decorated with a variety of filling patterns.

OUTLINE STITCHES
Any number of stitches can be used for outlining designs in addition to the simple back stitch variations shown here. Try working them in a thicker thread or combination of threads different from those used for the filling stitches. The stitches shown here are, from left to right, whipped back stitch, Pekinese stitch and threaded back stitch.

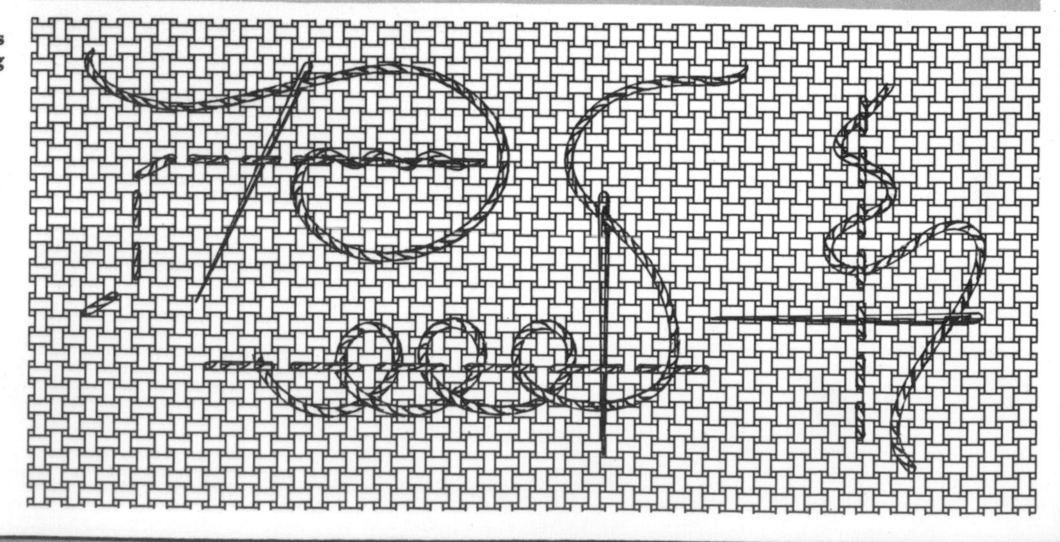

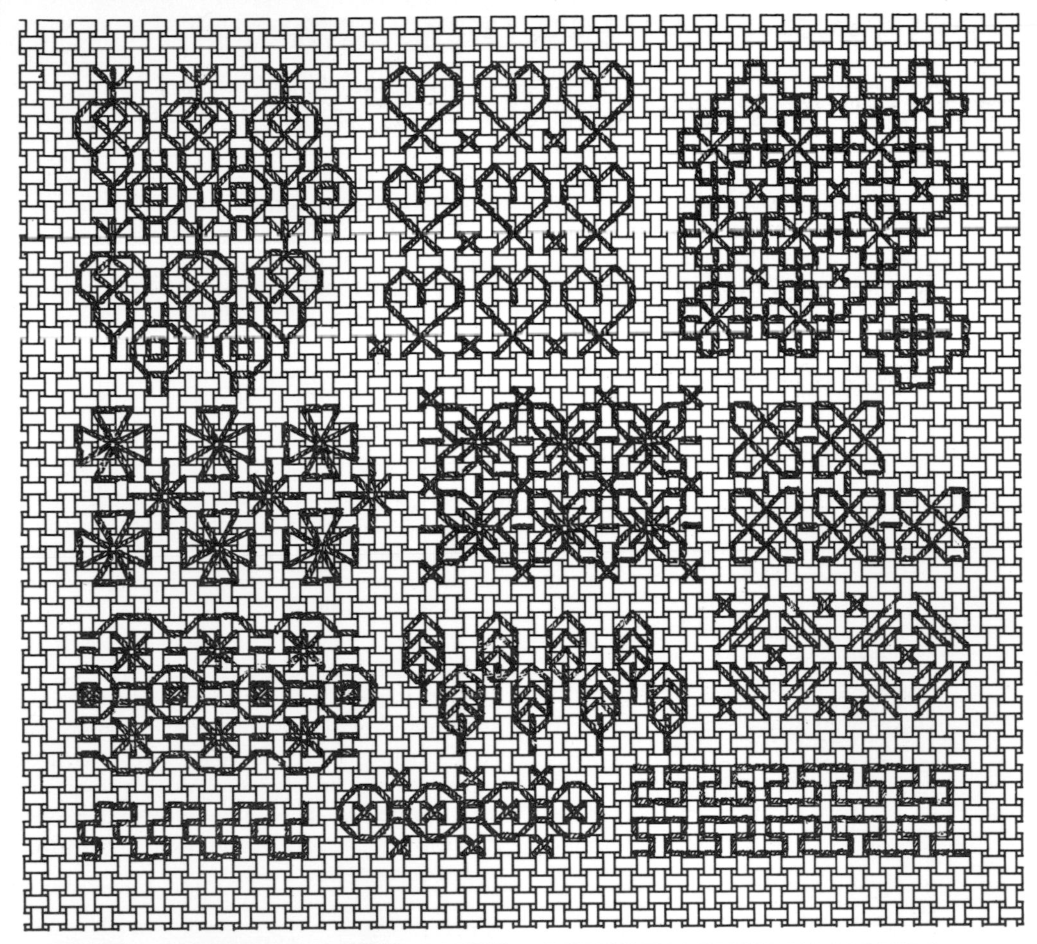

FILLING PATTERNS
There are an infinite variety of blackwork filling patterns. Before you begin to cover an area of fabric with a pattern, work one motif on a scrap of fabric to determine the scale of the pattern. Although the patterns shown here are worked over a specific number of threads, this may be too coarse or too fine for your fabric and thread.

BORDER PATTERNS
A single line from a filling pattern can be picked out and used for a border.

USING BLACKWORK MOTIFS AND PATTERNS

This twining vine design is an enlarged section of the coif shown on page 127. It makes an ideal design for a blackwork project. If, like the original embroiderer, you fill each section with a different pattern, you will be making a rich sampler as well. Use the four-part design for a cushion cover, or take only one circle of the vine and embroider it on some small item like a pincushion or a glasses case. Trace the area of the design that you want to embroider and enlarge it to the size required using the method described on page 124. Transfer the curving outline to the fabric and work this first, then fill in each area with a different pattern. For a simpler project, take one of the knot patterns (right) or any of the knots shown in the chapter and use it as a pattern. Enlarge or reduce it to size and then embroider it with a double line of any outline stitch and fill in each section of the knot with a different filling pattern. Use threads of different thickness to vary the density of the filling patterns.

APPLYING CANVASWORK SLIPS

Applying canvaswork slips to a fabric background is an amusing way of covering large areas of fabric with motifs.

HOW TO APPLY THE MOTIFS

1 If the finished article will not be subject to hard wear, trim away the canvas all around the embroidery, cutting right up to the stitches. Take great care not to cut through them. Pin and baste the embroidery to the background and sew all around it using the nylon thread.

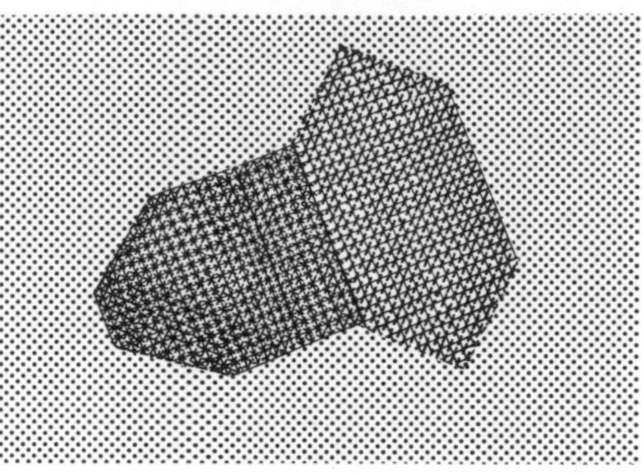

2 If the finished article will receive hard wear, trim the canvas to within ¼ inch (6mm) all around the embroidery. Clip into the corners and turn under the raw edges of canvas. Loose canvas threads will inevitably spring up and stick out, so oversew all around the canvas using a single strand of the same thread used to work the embroidery.

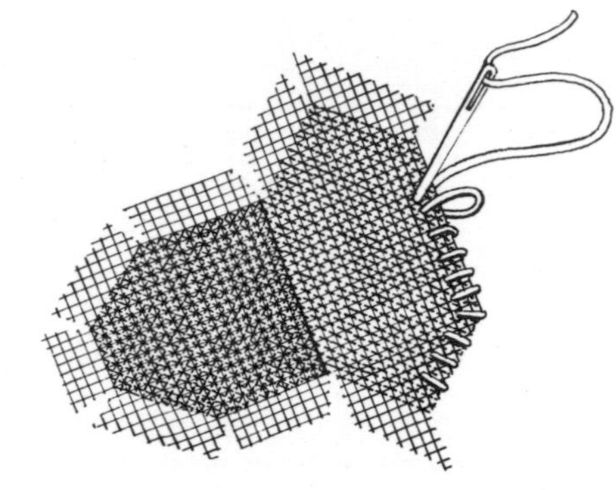

COUCHING ROUND THE SLIP

Outline the appliqué with a fine cord. Secure the cord on the underside of the fabric by oversewing it with tiny stitches. Take it through to the right side using a large-eyed needle. Couch the cord down with tiny stitches using invisible nylon thread. Take the cord to the underside of the fabric to finish.

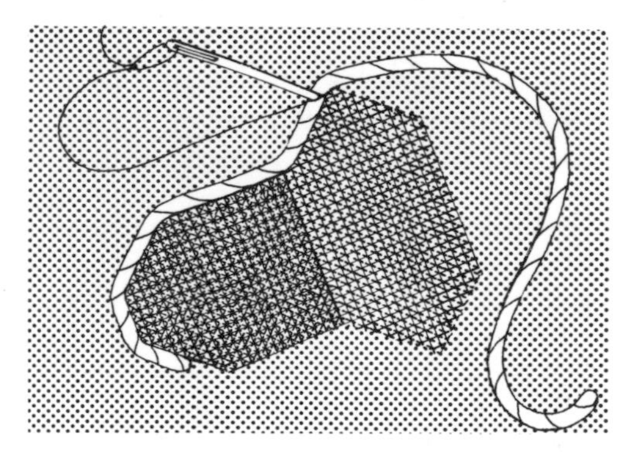

This form of embroidery is a beautiful way of covering a fabric with flower sprigs like the ones shown here. The slips can be used together with other embroidery techniques.

This form of appliqué is simple to do, but it does require neatness and patience. The edges of the canvas are neatened by a cord which is couched down all around the motif. Alternatively, you can work an embroidery stitch, such as stem or satin stitch around the edge. The final effect is rich and highly textured.

FABRIC

The applied canvas will be comparatively heavy, so choose a sturdy background fabric, backing it with muslin or a suitable interfacing for extra support if necessary. Good quality velvet or heavy linen are both suitable fabrics.

CANVAS

Work the embroidery on the finest canvas or evenweave linen that you can find and still work on comfortably. Canvas with 22 or 24 threads to the inch (44 or 48 threads to 5 cm) or even finer linen with between 26 and 34 threads to the inch (52 and 68 threads to 5 cm) are best.

THREADS

For the embroidery, use crewel wool, silk thread or stranded embroidery thread. To outline the appliqué and cover raw edges, twist any of these threads into a cord or buy a fine silk cord. Apply the embroidery to the background with invisible nylon thread. This makes it much easier to achieve a neat finish and the stitches do not detract from the embroidery. If you knot the thread into the eye of the needle, it will not slip out and is then no more difficult to use than ordinary sewing thread.

NEEDLES

As well as tapestry needles for the motifs, you will need a very fine sewing needle for the invisible thread and a large-eyed needle to take the cord through the fabric. You will also need a pair of fine sharp scissors to trim the canvas.

FRAMES

Work the motifs in a frame or not as you prefer, but be sure to block them before applying to the background. The appliqué must be worked with the background fabric stretched taut in a frame.

STUMPWORK

Stumpwork calls for ingenuity and imagination, for it combines a variety of techniques such as appliqué, canvaswork and bead work.

Although there are other forms of raised embroidery, for example, Victorian raised wool and plushwork, modern "soft sculpture" and three-dimensional work, stumpwork is much finer and more delicate than any of these.

FABRIC
The traditional fabric used for stumpwork was white satin. Use heavy furnishing satin, linen or cotton.

MATERIALS
Stumpwork allows you imagination in the choice of materials. In the seventeenth century, threads of wool, silk, cotton, gold and silver, beads and tiny seed pearls were all used. You will need a variety of such materials and also cotton padding, and fine florists' wire to use for three dimensional effects. Have a wide variety of needles available to use with these varied materials. You can also use a transparent glue to fix things in place if you find it easier than sewing.

TRANSFERRING DESIGNS
Use either the prick and pounce or the trace and baste methods explained on page 125.

FRAMES
Stumpwork must always be worked in a frame. The frame must be large enough to enclose the whole design as the raised stitchery must not be crushed. Choose a frame which will leave both your hands free to work the embroidery.

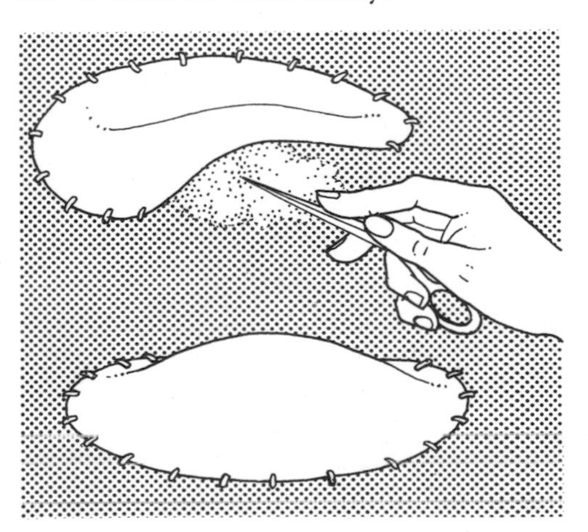

PADDING AND RAISING
Originally, raised embroidery was worked using wooden moulds. Canvaswork or embroidered material was applied on top of the mould or detached woven stitches were worked directly over the mould. You can still use balsa wood moulds to raise simple shapes if you can make them yourself, carving the wood with a craft knife; or use the methods shown below.

PADDING APPLIQUE
Cut out the appliqué slightly larger than the finished area of the design. If the appliqué is in canvaswork apply it using the method shown on page 130. If it is fabric, turn under the raw edges and sew it down to the background fabric using tiny stitches in matching thread. Leave a small opening along one side. Using your scissors, push cotton padding under the appliqué, moulding the embroidery into shape as you pad it, then sew down the opening.

PADDING WITH FELT
If you are going to embroider over the felt, it should be the same colour as the embroidery. Cut a piece of felt slightly smaller than the shape being padded. Cut three more pieces of felt, each slightly smaller than the last.

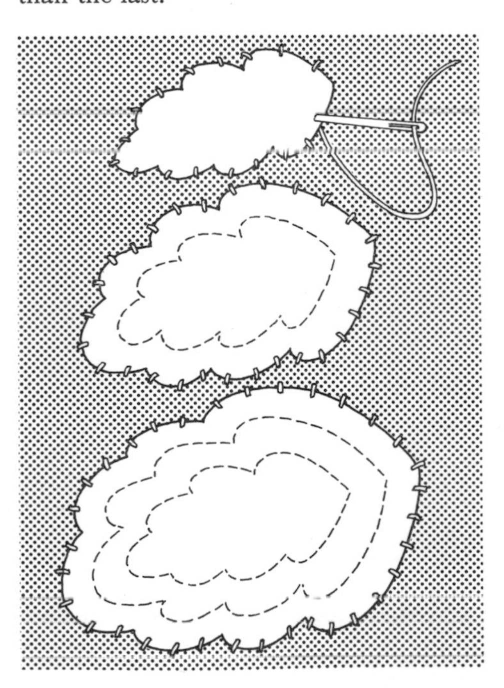

PADDING WITH FELT
Taking the smallest shape first, sew it to the fabric with tiny stitches. Keep the stitches close together to keep the edge of the felt from puckering. Sew the next layer of felt on top of the first, and then the largest layer on top of that. The felt is now ready to be covered with couching or detached filling stitches.

PADDING APPLIQUE
Far left: Cotton is pushed under the appliqué shape and the opening is then sewn down.

MAKING RAISED SHAPES OVER WIRE

Using this method, you can make simple shapes stand completely free of the background fabric. It is useful for making wings, leaves and petals. You will need a soft, easily bent wire like fine florists' wire, wire cutters and fine round-nosed pliers, like the ones used by jewellers. Use a fine embroidery thread with a firm twist. Twist a length of wire into the required shape using the pliers. Leave long ends of wire so that you can hold the shape while working embroidery over it, and so that the finished shape can be fixed in place on the underside of the fabric.

Wind thread closely over the wire. To secure the embroidery thread, using a crewel needle, slide the embroidery thread under a few of the wrapping threads and pull until the end is hidden. Then transfer the thread to a tapestry needle and work the embroidery. To fix the finished shape in place, first consider whether any surrounding embroidery should be worked on the background fabric before or after the shape is in place. Take the wire through to the wrong side of the fabric, holding the ends in place with tiny stitches.

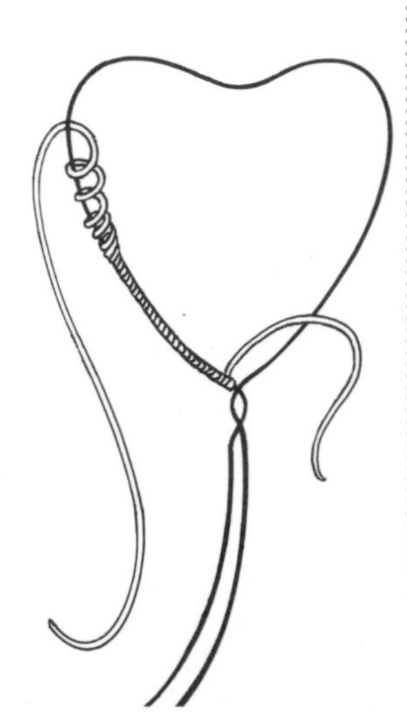

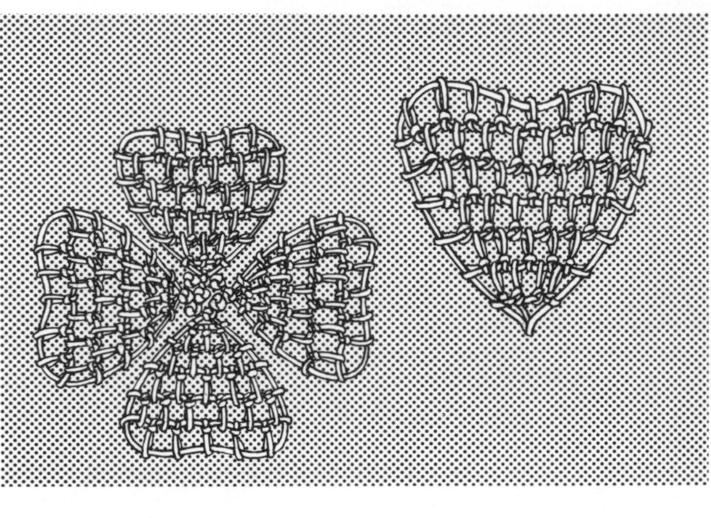

DETACHED FILLING STITCHES

Detached filling stitches are attached to the fabric only at the edges. Use them for covering padded and raised areas and for filling in wire frameworks. Use a fine thread and work the stitches closely together.

CEYLON STITCH
Left: Worked from a back stitch foundation, the finished stitch resembles knitting.

KNOTTED BUTTONHOLE FILLING
Centre: The needle only enters the fabric at the beginning and end of each row.

OPEN BUTTONHOLE FILLING
Far left: Work the first line directly onto the fabric.

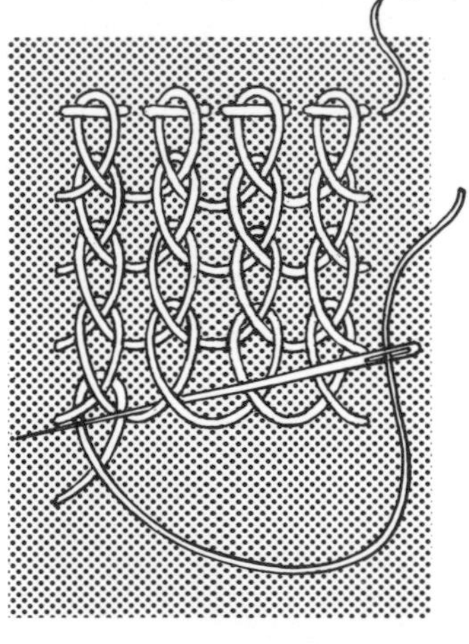

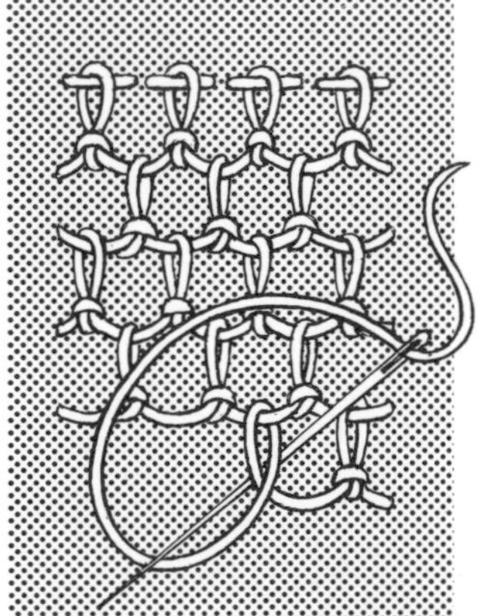

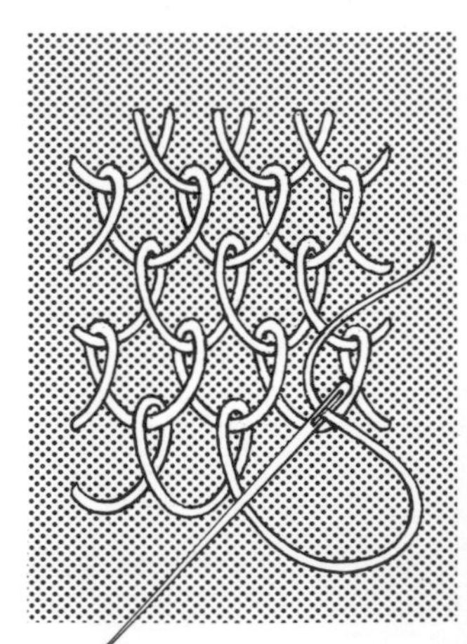

RAISED STITCHES

Many stitches can be used. Plush stitch (page 137) can be used cut or uncut; or work speckling stitches (page 128) loosely.

PADDED SATIN STITCH
Outline the motif in running stitch or chain stitch. Then fill in the whole area. Work satin stitch over these stitches first in one direction, then in another.

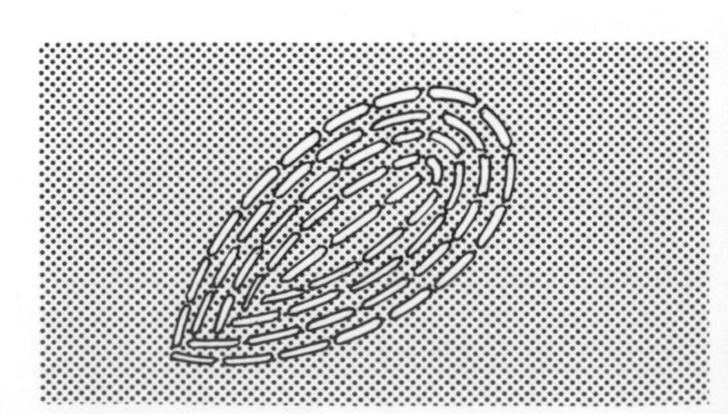

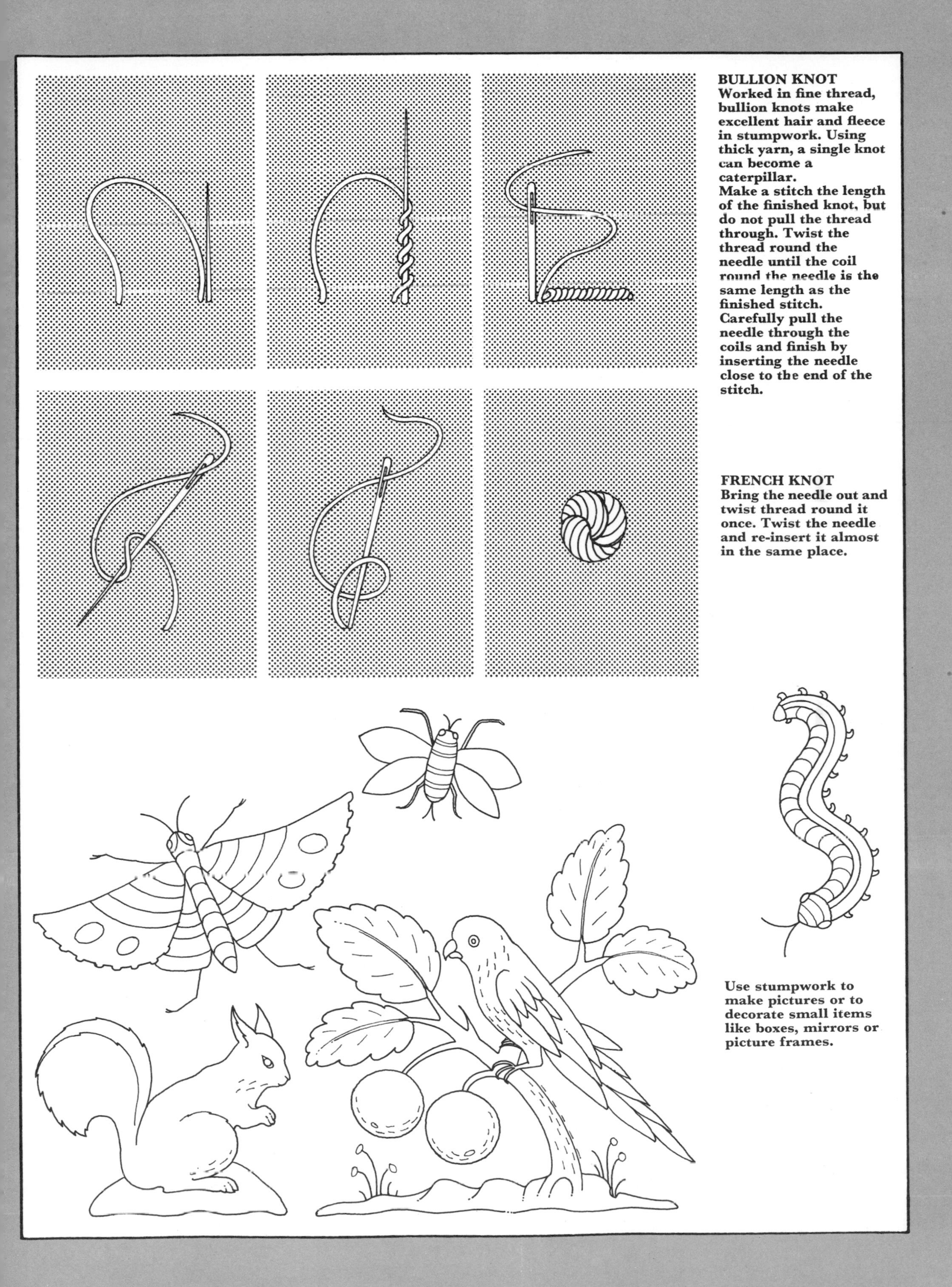

BULLION KNOT
Worked in fine thread, bullion knots make excellent hair and fleece in stumpwork. Using thick yarn, a single knot can become a caterpillar.
Make a stitch the length of the finished knot, but do not pull the thread through. Twist the thread round the needle until the coil round the needle is the same length as the finished stitch. Carefully pull the needle through the coils and finish by inserting the needle close to the end of the stitch.

FRENCH KNOT
Bring the needle out and twist thread round it once. Twist the needle and re-insert it almost in the same place.

Use stumpwork to make pictures or to decorate small items like boxes, mirrors or picture frames.

KNOTTING

Knotting is rarely seen today, however it is easy to learn and quick to work and has an attractive texture.

Simple overhand knots are worked at regular intervals on a length of thread by means of a shuttle. The thread is then couched down in patterns onto a background fabric. The technique is similar to the first steps in forming a tatting knot. Once mastered, it can be worked quickly and automatically. It requires practice to space the knots evenly, but you can soon learn to do this if you work slowly at first, slipping the thread off each finger in turn as you tighten the knot.

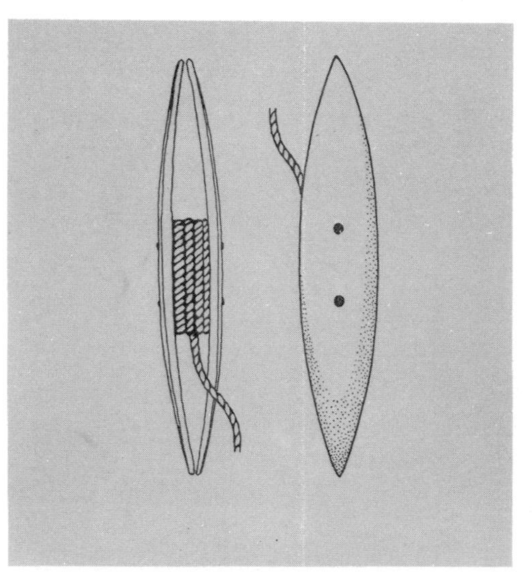

THE SHUTTLE

A small tool called a shuttle is required for knotting. Modern shuttles are made of plastic and measure about three inches (7·5 cm) long and one inch (2·5 cm) wide. Inside the shuttle is a small bar or reel. Fasten the thread by tying it to the bar. Wind the thread evenly round the bar until the shuttle is full.

THREAD

Fine, tightly twisted cotton thread, like crochet cotton is best, especially for learning. However, any thread can be used for knotting, even wool, as long as it is twisted. Soft embroidery thread or pearl cotton are good and make chunky knotted threads.

HOW TO WORK KNOTTING

1 Hold the free end of thread between thumb and forefinger of the left hand. Wrap the shuttle end round the fingers, under the little finger and hold next to the loose end between thumb and forefinger.

2 Hold the shuttle in the right hand and loop the thread over the left hand.

3 Take the shuttle under the thread from right to left.

4 Pull the shuttle through and slip the knot down between the finger and thumb.

5 A line of finished knots: To make the second knot, hold the first above the finger and thumb and repeat steps 1 to 4 over the first knot and then catching it between finger and thumb so as to form a new knot.

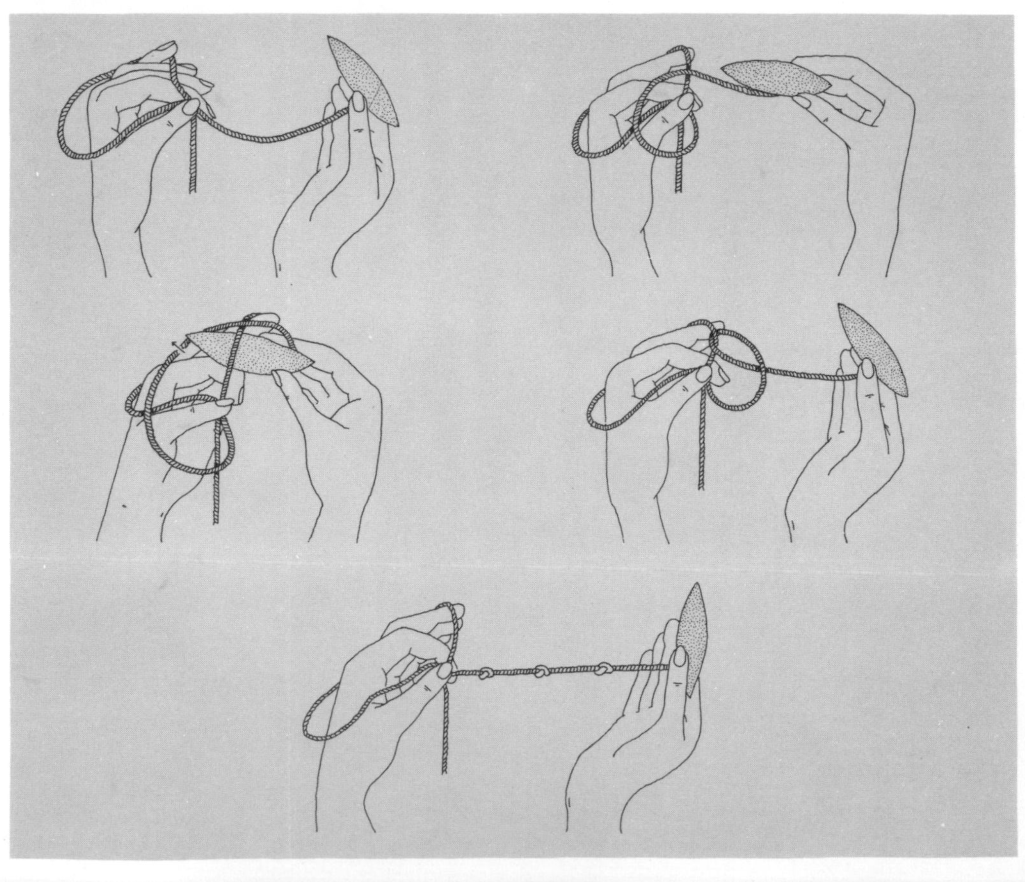

COUCHING

Outline the design on the fabric using any of the methods described on page 126. The fabric must be stretched taut in a frame. A rectangular frame is the best if the fabric will fit into it. For very large articles, or for couching on clothes, use a round frame and work only small areas of the pattern at a time. The knotting can be in the same colour as the background fabric for a subtle contrast of texture. Or lengths can be worked in different colours and used for different parts of a design.

As the knotted thread itself is decorative, the couching should be as invisible as possible. Use sewing thread the same colour as the knotted thread or use invisible thread. Take tiny stitches, sinking the thread in the knots, in the same way as that shown for couched cord on page 130. The couched thread can be used to outline a design or to fill in solid areas of pattern by couching threads close together in rows inside the outline of the design. In either case, begin and end by taking the end of the knotted thread through to the wrong side of the fabric with a large-eyed needle. Secure with tiny stitches.

The patterns for embroidery parterres are ideal for large items like bedspreads, and this technique is certainly the quickest way of working a rich textured pattern on a large piece of fabric. Sections of the pattern can be worked on cushion covers or on clothes. Knotting can be a very subtle way of decorating clothes if it is worked in fine thread only a few tones lighter than the background fabric.

Designs for parterres from *The Retir'd Gardener* **by George London and Henry Wise, 1710.**

BERLIN WOOLWORK

Berlin woolwork designs can be adapted today using a subtler and less strident range of colour than the originals.

Berlin woolwork is worked from a printed chart onto square mesh canvas. The designs are worked square by square and stitch by stitch from the chart.

CANVAS

Canvas is measured by the number of threads to the inch or to 5 cm. The finest canvas today has up to 34 threads to the inch (68 to 5 cm), and a coarse rug canvas can have as few as three threads to the inch (6 threads to 5cm). Choose the size of canvas according to what you want to make. For example, use fine canvas for small items like purses, bookcovers, glasses cases. For cushions or bags, a medium canvas with about 18, 16 or 14 threads to the inch (36, 32 or 28 threads to 5 cm) is best. For a large floor cushion or a rug, use rug canvas with a wide mesh. Canvas can be bought with single or double threads and either kind can be used for Berlin woolwork.

THREAD

Wool embroidery thread is used, although sometimes designs are highlighted with silk thread or beads. The type of wool you use will depend on the size of the canvas. It is most important that the wool covers the canvas adequately. If the wool is too thick for the mesh it will distort the threads of the canvas. If it is too fine, the canvas will show beneath the embroidery stitches.

The Palm Pattern, originally published in *The English Woman's Domestic Magazine*. **A selection of Berlin patterns are shown here and on the following pages. All would be suitable for rugs and cushions.**

Rug wool is the thickest wool, and crewel wool the finest. In between there are Persian wool and tapestry wool. Persian wool is very versatile as it comes in three strands which can be separated to use singly on fine canvas. Tapestry wool is almost as thick as Persian wool but it comes in a single strand which cannot be separated. Rug, tapestry and crewel wools can all be used with more than a single strand in the needle. Instead of using silk thread to highlight designs you can use stranded embroidery cotton as a contrast with the matt texture of the wool.

NEEDLES

Always use a blunt-ended tapestry needle which will pass easily between the threads of the canvas without splitting them. Needles range from size 13, the largest, suitable for rug wool; to size 26, the finest, suitable for a single strand of crewel wool. It is important that you choose the right size of needle to suit the canvas. If it is too small, it causes the wool to be dragged through the canvas at the point where it is doubled in the eye of the needle. A needle that is too large distorts the canvas threads. If in doubt about the right combination of canvas, wool and needle, ask for advice when buying the materials.

WORKING DESIGNS

Before you begin, mark the centres of the canvas horizontally and vertically with a line of basting stitches. Then find the centre of the design on the chart. In this way you can place the design centrally on the canvas. Begin working the design from the centre outwards. Always leave at least three inches (7·5 cm) of unworked canvas all around the embroidery to allow for making up the design. Plush stitch, which requires both hands to work it, must be worked with the canvas mounted in a frame, but you can work cross and tent stitch in the hand if you prefer.

The size of the finished design will depend on the size of the canvas mesh and also on the stitch used. For example, tent stitch is worked over a single intersection of the canvas thread while cross stitch can be worked over one or four intersections.

COLOUR AND PATTERN

Berlin designs often used four or five shades of each colour. Shading is particularly important in the realistic floral patterns like the circular pattern with roses shown on page 138. To shade roses realistically, look at real roses if possible, or keep a colour photograph by you while choosing the colours.

Contemporary taste in colour is vastly different from Victorian times, and you may even wish to simplify the designs by reducing the number of colours used. To work out colour schemes, transfer a section of the design to graph paper and colour in the different areas using crayons, or felt tip pens. Although the designs are clearly reproduced, you may find them easier to follow while embroidering if you transfer them to paper with larger squares. You need only transfer one quarter of the chosen design.

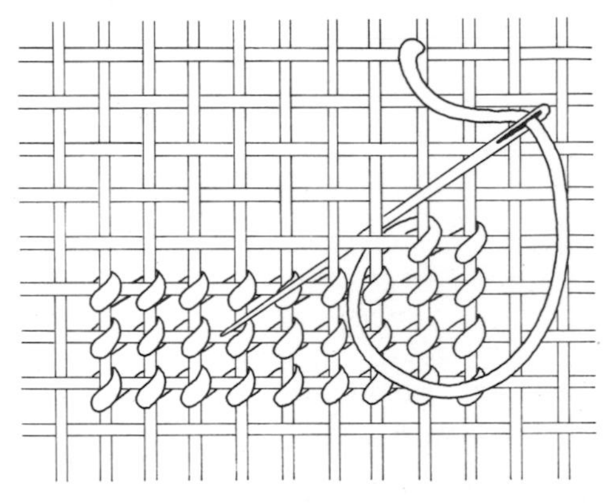

TENT STITCH
This is the basic canvaswork stitch. If the canvas is not mounted in a frame, it can be pulled out of shape by the diagonal slant of the stitching. The diagram shows tent stitch worked on single thread canvas.

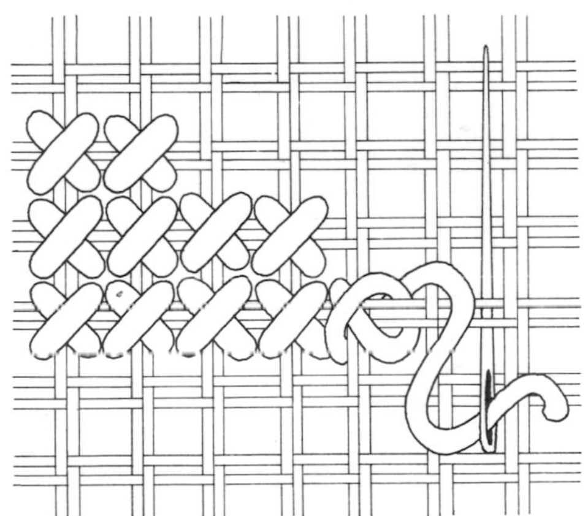

CROSS STITCH
Cross stitch should be worked so that all the stitches cross in the same direction. The diagram shows the stitches worked on double thread canvas.

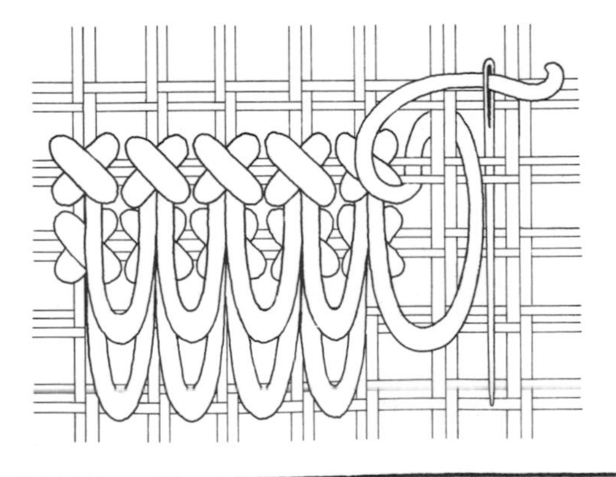

PLUSH STITCH
When the loops are cut, this stitch produces a raised pile. For best results, use a wool which fluffs easily. Work the stitches over a gauge—your finger, a knitting needle or a pencil, to ensure that the loops are even sized. Do not cut the loops until all the stitches have been worked. This stitch must be worked with the canvas mounted in a frame.

A long repeating pattern, originally designed for the welt around a chair seat.

This pattern and the one opposite were for circular footstools, but worked in modern colours they would make splendidly unusual cushions

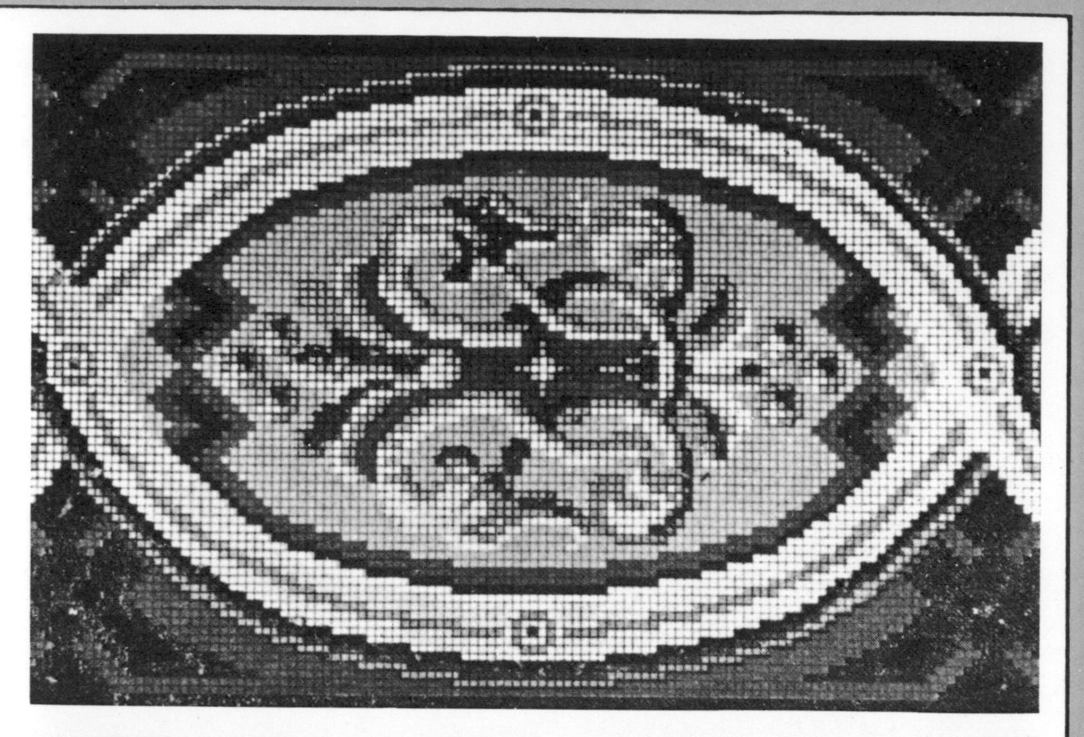

MODERN CANVASWORK

Whether in traditional or modern style, canvaswork is one of the most popular kinds of embroidery worked today.

With the wealth of materials and methods available, modern embroiderers are inspired in many directions. Raised embroidery can become three-dimensional "soft sculpture", blackwork can be used with the boldness of a newspaper photograph and collage combined with knotting. A popular trend today is to use a range of different stitches in a single piece of canvaswork, where in other ages, only one or two would have been used in combination. Certainly, one of the greatest interests of modern embroiderers has been texture and a greater freedom in the use of stitches. Many canvaswork stitches produce interesting textures when worked in combination and many can be worked in more than one thread to create effects from smooth and shiny to matt and fuzzy. It is this combination of a variety of stitches in an array of different materials that makes modern canvaswork so fascinating.

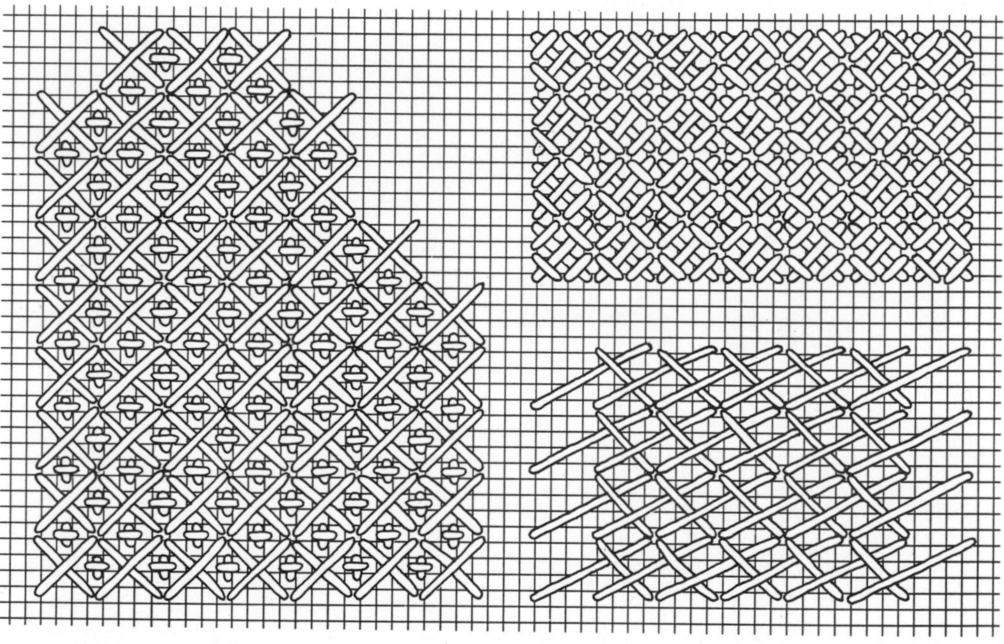

Right: Large cross and straight cross stitch. A combination of diagonal cross stitches worked over four threads of canvas with small cross stitches fitted into the spaces between.
Above: Rice stitch, also known as crossed corners and William and Mary stitch.
Below: Long armed cross stitch. Large areas of canvas can be covered quickly with this stitch.

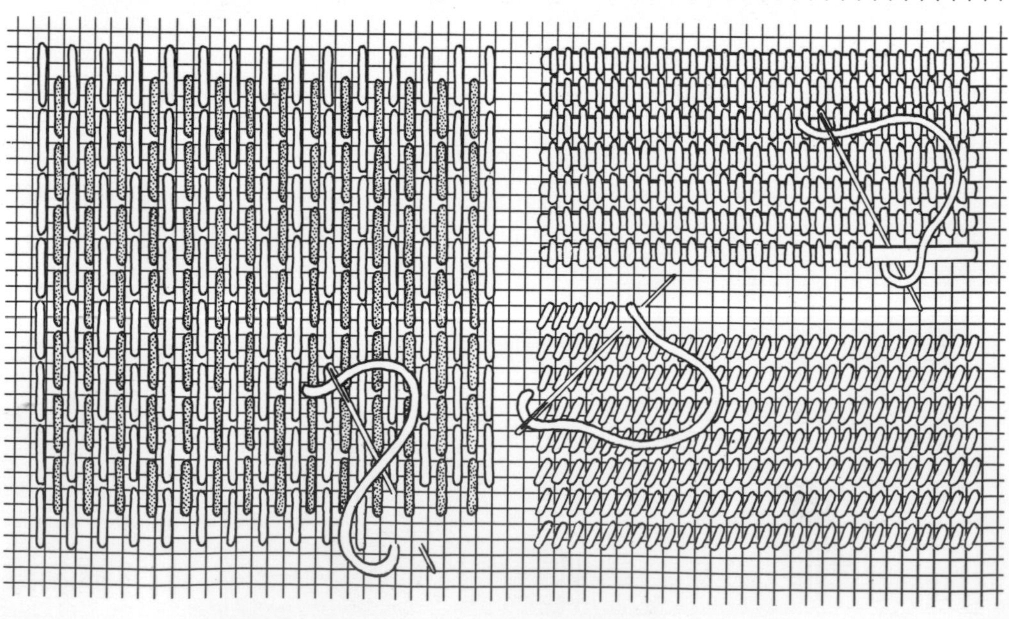

Left: Brick stitch.
Far left, above: Straight Gobelin stitch. Straight stitches are worked over a long padding stitch which hides the vertical canvas threads.
Below: Slanting Gobelin stitch.

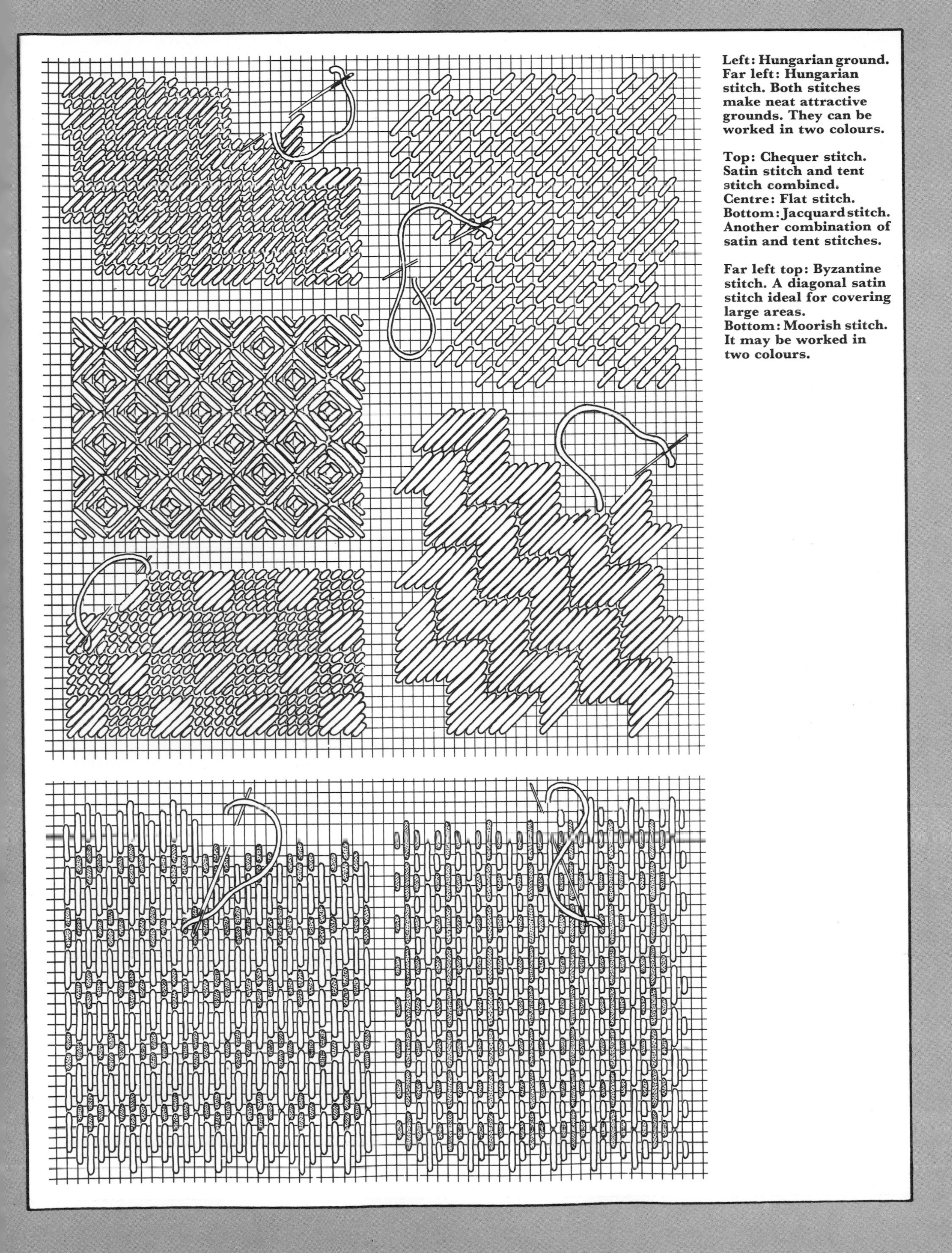

Left: Hungarian ground. Far left: Hungarian stitch. Both stitches make neat attractive grounds. They can be worked in two colours.

Top: Chequer stitch. Satin stitch and tent stitch combined. Centre: Flat stitch. Bottom: Jacquard stitch. Another combination of satin and tent stitches.

Far left top: Byzantine stitch. A diagonal satin stitch ideal for covering large areas. Bottom: Moorish stitch. It may be worked in two colours.

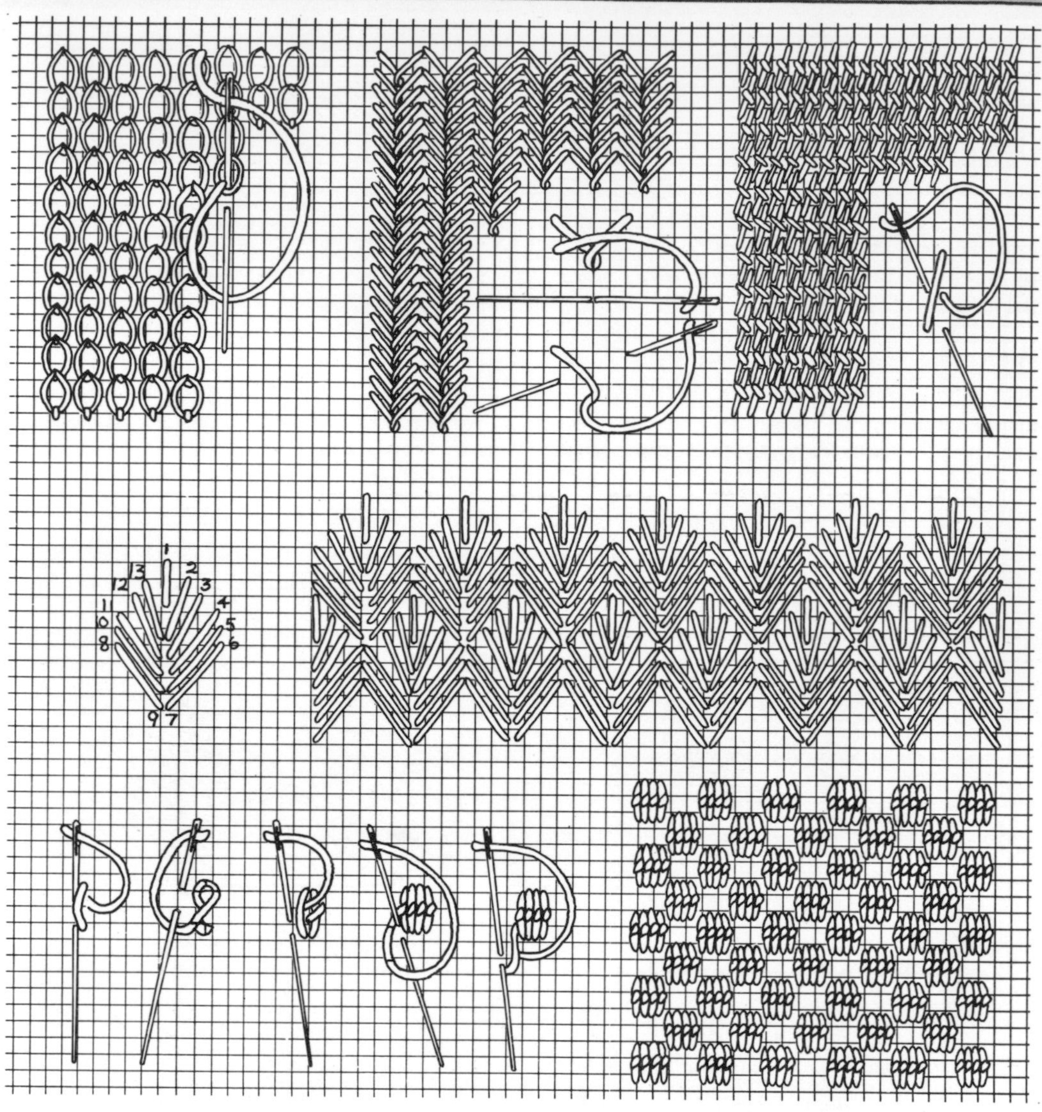

Right: Chain stitch. Each stitch is usually worked over one thread of canvas. Work all rows in the same direction.

Centre: Fern stitch. Work each row from the top downwards.

Far right: Knotted stitch. Rows of slanting stitches tied down in the middle.

Leaf stitch. Work each stitch in the order shown.

Rococo stitch. The groups of stitches are worked diagonally leaving small holes between. This stitch should be worked in a fine thread.

EMBROIDERING YOUR OWN GARDEN

The thought of embroidering your own garden is a tempting one, but perhaps it seems too daunting. However, the task is not so difficult if it is taken step by step. An embroiderer needs to work from a design with clear, bold and simple outlines. The details such as the shading of each flower centre and the texture of the grass, will be provided by the yarns and the stitches. So first concentrate on getting the essential elements of your garden down on paper—the shapes, their relationships to each other and the areas of light and shade. If you find drawing difficult here are two methods of tracing a design from your own garden, through a window and from a photograph, which will enable you to build up a design for your embroidered garden.

USING PHOTOGRAPHS

Take a photograph of your garden and have a large black and white print made. It is easier to produce an embroidery design from a black and white photograph as colour tends to confuse outlines. If the image is simplified into monochrome shades it is simpler to copy. Trace the area of the photograph that you want to use. To simplify the image even further, use a heavy, slightly opaque tracing paper over the print. Only the boldest shapes will show through and can be traced.

TRACING THROUGH A WINDOW

You can reproduce the view through your window in embroidery. You will need a sheet of clear plastic film like artists' tracing film or heavy duty plastic sheet, some adhesive tape and a felt pen that will write on the film.

Draw a "frame" on the film to the size you want the finished embroidery to be. If the window pane is not large enough, enlarge your tracing later. Find the place on the window where the view is framed to its best advantage and tape the film in place on the glass. Trace the outlines of the garden onto the film. Simplify the design by tracing shapes and shadows rather than the details of the scene.

DRAWING FOR EMBROIDERY

Many people who say that they cannot draw have never tried. If you are discouraged by your first attempts, use one of the suggested methods for the main outline of the design. Then go into the garden and make bold simple sketches of the elements you intend to include. Consider their basic shapes and structure and the effect of light and shade upon them. Look closely at the patterning in the bark of trees, the veining of leaves and ripples of water on a pool. Use these sketches to help you in translating the design into stitchery. The information from the sketches may suggest improvements in the main outline—or in the design of the real garden itself. It is an encouraging and pleasurable way to begin drawing and designing yourself.

A strawberry slip worked in a variety of stitches and yarns. The strawberries are worked in knotted stitch using stranded cotton, with French knot seeds. The calyxes in straight Gobelin stitch and the stems in chain stitch are worked in crewel wool, while the satin stitch leaves and Hungarian stitch background are worked in tapestry wool.

SELECT BIBLIOGRAPHY

GARDENS

Amherst, The Hon. Alicia. *A History of Gardening in England*. Quaritch: 1895.
Fairbrother, Nan. *Men and Gardens*. Hogarth: 1956.
Hunt, John Dixon and Willis, Peter. *The Genius of the Place: The English Landscape Garden 1620-1820*. Elek: 1975.
Hunt, Peter. (ed.) *The Shell Gardens Book*. Phoenix House: 1964.
James, Anne Scott and Lancaster, Osbert. *The Pleasure Garden*. John Murray: 1977.
Rohde, Eleanor Sinclair. *The Story of the Garden*. The Medici Society: 1932.
——. *The Old English Gardening Books*. Minerva Press: First edition 1924, reprinted 1972.
Thacker, Christopher. *The History of Gardens*. London Editions: 1978.

EMBROIDERY

Christie, A. G. I. *Samplers and Stitches*. Batsford: 1920.
Digby, G. F. Wingfield. *Elizabethan Embroidery*. Faber: 1963.
Edwards, Joan. *Crewel Embroidery in England*. Batsford: 1975.
Hackenbrock, Yvonne. *English and Other Needlework Tapestries and Textiles in the Untermeyer Collection*. Thames and Hudson: 1960.
Morris, Barbara. *Victorian Embroidery*. Herbert and Jenkins: 1962.
Swain, Margaret. *Historical Needlework*. Barrie and Jenkins: 1970.
Wardle, Patricia. *Guide to English Embroidery*. HM Stationary Office: 1970.

PICTURE CREDITS

The Metropolitan Museum of Art 1, 8, 15, 16, 17, 43, 44T, 48T, 58, 64, 83, 84.
Victoria and Albert Museum 10T, 11, 13, 16, 19, 22, 24, 27, 28T, 30T, 32TL, 32TR, 33T, 35, 38, 39T, 44B, 45, 47T, 50, 51, 52, 54, 55B, 57, 59T, 70L, 72T, 73, 77, 78, 79, 81, 85, 92, 93, 94T, 97, 99B, 104, 110, 120.
The Embroiderers' Guild Collection 90, 100, 108, 116.
The Bodleian Library, Oxford 9, 25.
The Ashmolean Museum, Oxford 23T.
Welbeck Estates Co. Ltd and Weidenfeld and Nicholson Archives 29.
Bowes Museum, Barnard Castle 20.
The National Portrait Gallery 69.
The British Library 37.
The British Museum 65TR.
Musée d'Art et d'Histoire, Genève 18B, 23B.
The National Trust Cover, 31, 67, 74T, 75.
The Linley Library 33B, 46, 94T, 103, 105.
Museum of Fine Arts, Boston 71.
Collection Ulster Museum 87T.
The National Gallery of Ireland 88B.
Mayorcas Ltd., Jermyn Street, London 14, 53T, 65B.
Mallet & Son (Antiques) Ltd., Bond Street, London 55T, 56, 68, 96.

Other illustrations are taken from books in private collections.

INDEX OF NAMES AND PLACES